# TORMOD

*Immortal Highlander Book 4*

HAZEL HUNTER

# HH ONLINE

Hazel loves hearing from readers!
You can contact her at the links below.

Website: hazelhunter.com

Facebook:
business.facebook.com/HazelHunterAuthor

Newsletter: HazelHunter.com/news

I send newsletters with details on new releases, special offers, and other bits of news related to my writing. You can sign up here!

# Chapter One

"ALMOST THERE, GAV," Jema McShane said, and squinted against the bleak mountain wind. She scanned the horizon before she helped her brother away from the car. "Isn't this a pretty spot?"

"Oh, aye, lovely," Gavin McShane said, as he gripped the handles of his rolling walker and glanced at the surroundings. "It's Baltic out here, you mad quinie."

Twilight crept up from the horizon as the late fall temperatures in the Scottish Highlands began a rapid plummet. In another hour they'd be courting hypothermia. Jema would have to be careful about how long she kept her brother out in the cold. Under his thick plaid woolens and trench coat, Gavin's joints and limbs had begun to resemble spindly kindling. His sluggish circulation made him chill easily. In his condition pneumonia was not only possible, it would be lethal. She'd misjudged how much time it would take to get him this far, but at least they were here.

Amyotrophic lateral sclerosis had been eating away at Gavin's brain and spinal cord for two years now. Because there was no cure for ALS, he wasn't expected to live far beyond three.

At least helping him along the dirt path from the makeshift parking lot to the Neolithic dig wasn't the ordeal she'd imagined. The grad students and volunteers working the site had carted out most of the heavy gear when they'd left for the day, packing the soil to a concrete hardness. Tomorrow they'd finish for the season by taking down the huts and collecting the cables and wires that provided power and lighting for the trenches.

How easy it was to ignore the fact that Gavin, who two years back had been a healthy beast of a soldier three times her size, now barely weighed two stones more than she did.

"Reminds me of those tyre graveyards they have in Kuwait," Gavin said sounding bored. But at least he was looking around them. "Is this what they do with ours now?"

"Not typically. Usually they grind up tyres and pave the roads with them. All of Europe does."

She tugged gently on his arm to bring him to a halt on top of the plywood. Active excavation units were surrounded with the broad, thin boards, keeping the pit walls from collapsing by dispersing the weight of the excavators. Slowly, she and Gavin turned the walker around so the seat faced the site. As she set the brakes, he all but fell onto the padded cushion. But when he realized she'd been watching him, he sat up straight and took the torch from her. She gave his shoulder a gentle squeeze before she stood aside.

A foot in front of them lay the last open trench at the site, where she had been doggedly trying to find any sign of the burial she felt sure was there. Hundreds of old car and truck tyres surrounded it on three sides, stacked and waiting for tomorrow. In the morning, the pit would be backfilled with soil and draped with tarps, which the tyres would hold down and cushion against heavy snow drifts. Though the smell of the old rubber baking in the sun had made her sick over the summer, now it just made her feel sad.

But she still had tonight, Jema told herself as she took off her backpack, lowered it over the side, and let it drop. She pulled off her down jacket.

"Keep the torch light on me while I climb down," she said. "You'll be able to see where I've been working." She eyed the plywood under the walker. "Don't move any closer to the edge. The soil there is dodgy."

Gavin watched her tuck her jacket over his legs. "You're off your head, you know. What if you have a fall? I'm not leaping to your rescue."

"You can still use a phone, you great hell-beast," Jema reminded him as she extracted her mobile, checked the signal and then placed it in his lap. "Dial one-oh-one if I keep screaming, or nine-nine-nine if I stop."

"Maybe I'll call for a cab." He glowered at her, which made her feel like she was seeing her reflection in his face. He had the exact same gray-blue eyes she had. "Be careful, Jay."

Jema grinned and kissed him on the brow. Gavin hadn't called her by her twin name in ages. "Ever and always, Gee."

The short ladder extending down into the trench had been hand-painted with a V-9, designating it the ninth trench in which they'd found Viking-Age artifacts. The most exciting, an ax-head still attached to a piece of wood handle, had been tentatively dated back to the first century BCE. Radiocarbon dating on the organics would be done back at the laboratory, but Jema wasn't interested in the weapon—it's what it might indicate.

V-9 was a burial pit. Jema would swear to it.

Of course, they hadn't yet found a grave, or remains, or any indication that a body had been buried here. Initially the trench had been filled with roots from several ancient, enormous oak tree stumps they'd found on the surface, which had made excavating it tricky. Jema had read several articles which speculated the Vikings deliberately planted trees over such graves in order to disguise and protect the dead, but she wasn't sure if she agreed. For one thing the tree stumps had been massive. When the tree ring dates came back, she wouldn't be surprised if they'd been planted a thousand years before the burial would have taken place.

The moment they had begun digging out the trench, however, Jema had begun feeling the oddest sensations. Her skin became acutely sensitive, while her heartbeat seemed to slow down. Whenever she touched a stone or root her fingers seemed to pulse with some frantic energy. She kept seeing in her mind the crude drawings she had studied depicting Freyja's Eye, even when she didn't want to think about them. She knew all of it was unprofessional, possibly delusional, and would get her thrown off the dig if she told anyone about it. So Jema had kept it to herself while she continued digging.

Now she reached the bottom of the trench and stepped off the ladder before waving and calling up to Gavin, "I'm in."

"You're daft," he called back, but kept the light from the torch trained on her. "There's nothing down there I can see. It's not but a big hole in the ground."

"That's because you're a soldier, not an archaeologist," Jema said and pointed to the feature she'd uncovered last week. "This is an inner wall face. The stones used to build it are these slab-like rocks called orthostats. They were stacked in parallel and vertical positions to create slots."

"Slots?" Gavin said and frowned down at her. "Like a casino?"

"No, like keyholes…or air holes." She took out a dental tool from her backpack and gently inserted the tip into one of the slots until it almost completely disappeared. "I feel something on the other side of this. It may be a created space, like a burial chamber."

He leaned forward to peer over the edge. "What, then, you want to unlock a grave?"

"Be careful," she said and eyed the position of his feet. "Don't put weight near the lip of the unit or the sidewall might give way." They'd already removed the stabilizing boards around the base of the pit. "You'll fall on top of my great discovery."

"A grave with slots," he mocked as he sat back.

"Or the final resting place of Freyja's Eye," Jema said and moved the probe to test another space. "Can you imagine it? A golden diamond the size of your fist, carved to honor the goddess's own beautiful eyes. Although it probably isn't even a diamond. It might be a fist-sized topaz, or a hunk of polished amber."

"Which can also use sunlight to melt off your face," Gavin put in. "Don't forget that part. I've not, since you told me."

"That's just another myth," she assured him. "The Vikings always exaggerated their legends to strike fear in the hearts of their enemies. There's another one that says for every enemy that the Eye kills, it also takes the life of a loved one."

"So that's where they got that eye-for-an-eye thing," Gavin said and rubbed his brow. "I always thought that came from the Bible."

"No, it's actually from Hammurabi's Code," she told him. "Mesopotamian king of Babylon, and not a particularly forgiving man. You would have liked him."

Her brother made a rude sound. "Stop

showing off how brilliant you are. Why are you so obsessed with this bloody rock? You can't sell it or keep it."

Her heart twisted as she shrugged and removed the probe. "The Eye will go to the National Trust, to be worshipped by countless generations of kids forced on museum outings. The find, however, would be mine. A discovery of that magnitude would get me a publication in every archaeological journal in the world. Edinburgh would finally offer me a full-time teaching position."

Gavin uttered a short laugh. "You hate Edinburgh."

She did, but that didn't matter. "I could take a flat for us near the uni, and get a home carer to look after you while I'm at work. You remember the doctor there who is testing that new drug treatment–"

"Jema, I'm going to die, and soon, and it won't be pleasant." He stared down past her. "Unless I can make it happen faster, and cleaner."

*He was talking about ending himself,* Jema thought, and swallowed a surge of bile. "No, Gavin. That isn't the way."

"Why not?" he asked her, a strange intensity in his voice now. "I roll over the edge, fall into your pit, and break my neck. Fast and clean."

"Unless you don't break your neck, and end up a quadriplegic with ALS," Jema retorted. "You're a barrel of giggles, Gee. Bedridden on a respirator, not that much."

She shook her head and clenched her teeth to keep from saying more. Talk of the end of her twin brother's life had not been the reason she'd brought him. Somehow she'd thought he'd be as excited about the dig as her. Quickly she turned away from him but as she did her heel caught. Without time to brace her fall, the back of her head bounced off stone slabs in the trench wall. As she landed hard in the corner, the air whooshed from her lungs and dirt landed in her face.

"*Jema*," Gavin yelled. "You all right? Answer me."

She frantically brushed the soil from her eyes to find the light from the torch swinging back and forth over her head. Her lungs ached but she managed to draw in a long breath before she coughed.

"Jema, I'm calling for help!"

"No," she gasped and cleared her throat. "No!"

She pushed herself up, the dental tool pushing painfully into her palm. She gripped it as she struggled to her knees then clambered to her feet.

"I'm fine," she called up to her brother, and silently winced as she touched the back of her head. She squinted into the torch light. "Don't call anyone. Oh, damn, damn, damn."

"Are you hurt?" her brother demanded.

She held up her other hand to shield her eyes. "Yes," she hissed, her fingers probing the tender spot on the back of her head. At least she didn't feel any blood.

"What's that in your hand?" Gavin asked.

"It's my…" She'd been about to say 'probe', but the glitter of gold stopped her. Instead of her tool she was staring at a dirt-crusted, golden torque set with orange gems. "What the… Where did…" She glanced down at where she had fallen. "Gee, aim the torch down there!"

Delicate silver links pocked the dirt, and ended in a large disc sticking up from the ground. Both took on a silvery glow as sparkling light came from some roots sticking out of the wall she'd hit.

Jema reached a shaking hand for the disc.

"What is it?" Gavin called down, as his walker scraped across the wood.

As she blinked at the gleaming find, her subconscious registered the fact that he was moving. She spun toward him.

"No, Gee, stay where you are." The ground began to rumble under her feet, and she shouted, "Move back from the trench. Gavin, move *now*."

But as the words left her Jema saw the ladder tilt at a crazy angle and the wall in front of her collapse. Her brother fell from his seat and pitched forward. She dropped the torque as she reached up, hoping she could catch him without breaking his bones or hers. Then the world disappeared from under her feet, and she was sucked into a terrifying void.

Oak tree roots stretched around her, encircling her as she tumbled over and over, unable to see or stop herself by grabbing a handhold. She screamed for Gavin, and saw him above her, his body encased in the same light that had come from the tree roots.

*We're going to die,* Jema thought. *No one will realize we're gone. It was only us two.*

She finally struck bottom, but there was no bottom, only a tangle of more roots. She clawed her way through them to collide with another wall of stone, this one slamming into the side of her face. As consciousness ebbed, the warmth of blood streaked across her face. Numbly, Jema gave herself to the cold dark that surrounded her, and discovered one final surprise—she was grateful.

Gavin didn't have to die alone.

# Chapter Two

ON THE EDGE of a dense, massive forest in the Scottish Highlands, Tormod Liefson dismounted from his white gelding and took in his surroundings. The last rays of sunset shimmered on the horizon. He'd need light to continue on. Tethering the horse to a bush near some good graze, he picked up a long branch, fashioned it into a torch with rag-wrapped touchwood, and used his firesteel to light it.

"'Tis the place," he told the gelding. "I ken it."

The horse grunted and shook its head as if to disagree.

Tormod pulled from his pack the map

fragment he'd unearthed from an ancient battlefield. "Three peaks and a crooked valley," he said holding up the tattered hide with its faded markings to compare them to the same features beyond the forest. "Timber land with no settlements or roads near. Too steep for herds, too cold to farm. Ten leagues from the site of the last Viking battle with the Cruthin. 'Tis where they'd want to bury a great warrior like Thora."

The gelding dipped its head and began cropping grass.

"What do you ken? You're a nag." Tormod carefully rolled the hide and tucked it away before he shouldered the pack. A pang of guilt made him rub the gelding's withers. "Aye, and I'm a fool."

He had ten hours before he was expected back at Dun Aran for guard duty, but it would take him three to ride back to the Red Ox to stable the gelding and return to Skye. Seven hours to find a grave that had been hidden for over a thousand years in a forest so wide and deep it would take a week simply to cross it on foot.

*If* the map proved accurate.

Tormod had been searching for this grave ever since hearing the legend of Thora the Merciless. Unlike the Pritani, Vikings revered women who chose the warrior's path. Called shieldmaidens, they had lived short and brutal lives waging war alongside their husbands, brothers and fathers. Thora's fierce reputation for slaughtering every Pritani who came within reach of her blade had prompted the tribes to offer an enormous bounty for her head or her surrender. None had ever collected on it. Thora's loyal men were said to have spirited her body away after she had bled to death from her wounds.

Songs were still sung about Thora the Merciless who had chosen death over surrender.

From the forest edge Tormod walked into the trees, making his way north through the brush. After an hour he crossed what appeared to be an old dirt path that curved to the south, and which bore dozens of deer tracks. He knelt down and brushed back the moss and rotting leaves to expose the soil, which had hoof ruts. When he took a pinch to taste, that explained why the trail wasn't overgrown. It had been salted.

He could guess how Thora's men had guarded against grave robbers. The path would lead to a cleared patch of land with a square of carved runestones inside a larger ring of oak stumps. The stones, carved with the four harpoons of the Svefnthorn, would be imbued with the power of a shamanic warrior. Svefnthorn cursed anyone who stepped into the clearing to sleep forever.

"You canny bastarts," Tormod muttered. He ignored the path and continued north, his steps quickening.

As expected the trees grew thicker, and then became tall white oaks deliberately close-planted so they would graft together. Their pleached limbs formed a living barricade so effective that his torch flame barely flickered. But he also knew that her men would have returned to honor her. He slowed his pace around the wall of oak and still almost missed it. A small, baffled entrance appeared, cleverly set back and barely deep enough for him to step in. Nose almost on the inner wall of boughs, he side-stepped along the barrier, the torch illuminating the new narrow corridor—until he was in.

A broad oval of sweet woodruff spread out before him, its tiny white flowers perfuming the air with the scent of newly-mown hay. He grinned at the familiar aroma. If they had buried Thora here, they would have first put down a layer of bedstraw. But his tribe had also used dried sweet woodruff to stuff their mattresses. He'd gathered it for his mother every spring. The weed sometimes sprouted inside the ticking. Like his tribe, it was almost impossible to kill.

Tormod Liefson, son of Arn and Gilda, map-maker and immortal warrior, would always be a Viking.

Pride bloomed in his chest at the thought that Thora had earned a warrior's burial. She'd led devastating raids against the Caledonians, the Britons and even the Danes, making her warriors some of the wealthiest men in Norrvegr. Her greatest triumph had come just before her death, when she had destroyed an entire fleet of enemy ships after they had destroyed hers.

But Tormod remembered the greatest

female Viking warrior not as a shieldmaiden, but as the child she had been. To him Thora Liefson would always be the impish little sister who had put frogs in his boots.

He stopped short of the center of the little meadow, and lowered his torch, moving it from side to side until he caught a glimpse of smooth stone.

"I vowed to find you, and bring you back to sleep beside our parents. Permit me to keep my word tonight, Sister."

An owl answered him with a hooted cry before flying off into the oaks.

He planted his torch and knelt down, pulling back the flower-spangled runners until he found the first ship stone.

"Much has changed since you fled Skye, Thora. I was captured and enslaved, but the Pritani didnae treat me cruelly. Some years later I fought with them against Romans hunting druid kind. For my efforts my master freed me from slavery."

Though he knew she couldn't hear him, the telling of his tale was somehow comforting. He described the ugly end he and the McDonnel clan had met, but then how he'd been wakened to immortality. As Tormod unearthed more stones he rambled on about his life as a guard and map-maker to the clan.

"We've a thought-reader at Dun Aran. She and Evander married last winter. That was long after he turned traitor but just after he saved the clan. He's Captain of the Guard now."

After a thousand years he knew that little would remain of her, but his vow did not permit him to stop his search. None of the McDonnels knew of his quest, and the laird would hardly approve. But as the last reminder of what he had been before his enslavement, bringing his sister's remains back to Skye would help keep him from turning into a facking Scotsman.

"What more would you have me tell you?" he asked the ground as he cleared off the final stone. Along with the others they had been arranged in the shape of a ship's hull, but now lay in a tumbled pile. "I could tell you of the druid women from the future who keep falling into our midst and bringing their strange ways to the clan. Diana, our cop, has me running through the Black Cuillin like a hunted stag every morn. You'd like her. Red doesnae suffer fools or kiss arse. If she hadnae given her heart to Tharaen Aber…but she did, and that's done." He sat back on his haunches and pressed his hand to the ground. "I only wish I could bring you back, little sister."

The moss shuddered under his palm.

Tormod jumped to his feet as the oaks around the clearing stirred. Under his boots the ground rumbled, and then shook, nearly felling him. The stones marking the grave began to glow like miniature moons, and then the clearing exploded with a fountain of rock and earth.

*"Jema,"* a man's voice bellowed from inside the grave.

Reaching up to cover his head, Tormod instead caught a body that hurtled out of the ground and into his arms. The impact knocked him on his arse, and he bowed over the form as soil and broken stones rained down to pelt them. At last the madness stopped, and he straightened to look down at the unconscious woman in his grasp.

Blood from a gash on her brow trickled into her long hair, which streamed from her head and over his arm like a small silken river of fiery gold. She wore a thin bodice with the words I'D RATHER BE DIGGING printed on it, and trews made of faded indigo cloth. Her boots were a marvel, but Tormod couldn't stop looking at her face. Even covered in blood and dirt, he could see that she wasn't his sister brought back to life. Thora had been dark-haired and brown-eyed, like their mother.

This woman was fashioned from his dreams.

Gently he placed her on the ground, and hoisted himself up to go over and look into the ragged pit in the ground. Huge tree roots laced the perimeter of the deep pit, which contained nothing but mounds of dirt. Since Thora's men would have buried her with weapons and other grave gifts to serve her in the afterlife, the stones must have been a lure to another spell trap.

But why would a woman be flung through it? He glanced back at her and then back at the grave, thinking on the women he'd just been describing. Had the trap been laid atop an ancient oak grove, and activated a time portal?

Tormod heard the woman choke, and went back to kneel beside her. "'Twill be well, my lady."

She convulsed, coughing and writhing as she tried to push herself upright. He helped her into a sitting position, and brushed the soil from her face. She had silvery blue eyes framed by dark gold lashes, and an angular face with the whitest, most flawless skin he'd ever seen.

After another spate of coughing and blinking she focused on Tormod's face, and her fine brows drew together.

"Where am I?" she whispered hoarsely. "What happened?"

"I wish I could tell you," he said. She sounded Scottish, which perplexed him. All the other women who had crossed over had come from a place called San Diego, and spoke with the same, blunt accent. "You were flung up from that pit into my arms."

Her eyes shifted toward the jagged hole in the ground. "I was?" She stared at him. "Why?"

"I cannae tell you, but know that you…are safe here, with me." Tormod felt like an addled boy for staring at her, but he couldn't stop himself. "I'm called Tormod Liefson." She squinted at him, as if trying to make sense of what he said. "Map-maker of the McDonnel Clan," he added quickly. "I came here to…map the place."

"Ah, it's grand to meet you, Tormod. I'm…" She winced and lifted her hand to gingerly touch her wound. "I'm hurt."

"Aye." He shifted with her so the light from the torch better illuminated the gash, which still oozed blood. Using his sleeve, he blotted the worst away and inspected it again. "'Tis no' so bad. It wants cleaning and bandaging is all." He'd have to attend to it, and quickly, for the smell of mortal blood could attract the undead.

"That's good," she said but didn't sound relieved, only more worried. She looked around them again. "What did you say this place is?"

The forest had no name that Tormod knew, and to tell her she'd crossed through time to land in the distant past would only frighten her.

"You're in the highlands, in the woods." Suddenly he recalled the word he'd heard shouted from the grave. "Are you named Jema?"

Her mouth worked, shaping the name in silence, and then panic flooded her face and she clutched at him. "I don't know. I can't remember. My name, where I was, how…" She shook her head a little. "I can't remember *anything*."

Tormod covered her hands with his, and still felt them under his palms as her face and body grew insubstantial. He could see through her to the torn sweet woodruff under her, the tiny white flowers showing plainly through her face. A moment later he still held her hands, but could not see her at all.

"What is happening to me?" her voice asked as her invisible hands tightened on his tunic.

## Chapter Three

GAVIN MCSHANE CAME out of darkness into darkness, and instinctively waited for the pain to blaze up his legs into his groin. The damage ALS had done to his spine caused near-constant muscle contractions in his calves and thighs, which triggered cramps so intense he often vomited from the pain. Any unusual amount of physical activity, like hobbling out to Jema's dig, aggravated the spasticity attacks. He'd be in agony any moment.

Except there was nothing. All he felt was dirty, chilled, and a little disoriented.

Sitting in the facking dirt, and yet feeling grand as a brigadier. It had to be the adrenalin. Soon it would wear off and he'd pay. Oh, how he'd pay for the fall. He took in a deep breath of frigid air, and felt his chest expand like a huge bellows. He hadn't been able to breathe like that since… No, it couldn't be.

Not after two years of living like an old man.

Gavin's eyes adjusted to the darkness. Even ill he'd always had excellent night vision. What he saw when he looked down at himself made him utter a short laugh. It was ludicrous. Yet when he stretched out his arms—his long, strong arms—he felt the power he'd once possessed coiling in his muscles. He drew up his forearms and saw his biceps bulge. The biceps that had vanished on him entirely were now as big as melons.

Accepting that he was sick, diseased, beyond hope—a dying man with no chance of improvement or recovery—had been a battle. This transformation was insanity.

Gavin brought his hands to his chest, which stretched wide under the ragged remains of his shirt. His wasted legs felt like unshakeable marble columns as he rose to his feet. Even in the dark he could see his body now looked exactly as it had when he'd been in the best shape of his life, during his military service as a captain in The Black Watch.

But as he gazed down at his new form, a thought gave him pause.

*Am I dead?*

He'd fallen into that trench, where he must have broken his neck, and now he was beyond all that. Was this his reward, his afterlife?

He took a stride, and then another, stopping only when he nearly smacked face-first into a tree. Turning around, he peered at the woods surrounding him, which looked nothing like his sister's dig site.

*Jema.*

"Jema!" he screamed, his voice echoing as if he were standing in a giant cavern. "Jema!"

When no response came he went back to the spot where he'd woken. The ground appeared slightly hollowed, as if he'd dropped there, but he saw no sign of his sister or her dig. The entire area appeared heavily wooded and untouched. He remembered the ground shaking and Jema screaming.

His hands balled into fists and his temper frayed like the strands of a rotted rope. Where was his sister?

Something wet splatted on Gavin's face, and when he looked up a curtain of icy rain poured over him, knocking the breath out of his lungs. He ran for cover, ducking under the thick branches of a tall oak and pressing himself against the rough trunk. His anger billowed, and then his big body seemed to heat up like a furnace. He felt raindrops sizzling on his skin, and glanced down to see his chest now covered in oak bark.

"Shite."

He reached for his chest, only to see his hand covered in the same rough material. Fear surged through his fury, and he shoved away from the tree to run back out into the icy rain. As lightning flashed overhead, he watched his flesh return to its smooth dark tan—a tan he'd lost three years back after being discharged from the military. What was happening to his body?

"Hell's fucking bells," he muttered as he looked up at the bleak night sky. His eyes filled with rain as he shouted at the God he stopped believing in long ago. "What more have you done to me now, you evil old bastard?"

He didn't wait for an answer. Whatever

had happened, he would have to sort it out later. Now he had to find his sister. He trotted in a search pattern, moving in an ever-expanding circle around the spot where he'd regained consciousness. Frosty rain pounded over him, but Gavin barely felt it as he looked for any sign of Jema or the dig. As the sky lightened and the storm abated he studied the trees. The wide trunks, heavy coverings of moss and deep layer of leaf rot on the forest floor told him this area hadn't been disturbed for decades, possibly centuries.

His big body may have been restored to its former physical perfection, and no longer suffered from wet or cold, but Gavin could feel the burn of the unaccustomed exertion in his muscles. He'd be of no use to his sister if he dropped from exhaustion. Using the North Star as a marker for true north, he headed in that direction.

Though the rain stopped, the cold wind made his soaked clothes feel like a shroud of ice. Even so, it didn't seem to affect Gavin's body temperature. He wondered if he'd grown feverish, and stopped at the first stream he found to splash his face. Drinking the water without a filtration or sterilization kit was beyond foolish, but he was thirsty. If he was already dead, it wouldn't matter. He cupped his hand to drink from it, and the water tasted so icy it made his teeth ache.

When he looked up he saw a gray-faced red deer on the other side of the stream, watching him with its big dark eyes. Its ears flicked as it lowered its muzzle into the stream and drank.

"I can't be your afterlife," Gavin said, and then watched the deer bound into the trees, just as the first rays of dawn sparkled on the water.

On the other side of the stream stood a rough-looking cottage that he recognized as a hunting lodge. Jema had shown him countless pictures of one she'd helped reconstruct during another dig she'd worked on as a student. She and the other helpers had built it based on measurements taken from a few rotted stumps they'd uncovered around a pile of animal bones.

"Hello?" Gavin waded across the stream and went to the door of the lodge, hammering on it with his fist. "Anyone in? I need help."

After several minutes of silence, he used a shoulder to force in the door, and stepped inside to find the only room inside deserted. A primitive table and chairs sat to one side of a huge fireplace, in which a blackened caldron hung over a pile of ashes. Another table held a collection of crude tools, sharp-ended pegs, an uneven roll of cording, and bits of leather and hide. The door to an apparent cellar was off to one side. What he didn't see was any telephone, lights, switches or appliances. The one window had no glass in it, and was so narrow it bordered on a slit.

The place appeared too well-built to be a shelter cobbled together by a drifter or poacher. Could it be one of the university reconstructions Jema had worked on?

Gavin retrieved an old blue and green tartan from a pallet made of rope and branches that had been piled with straw. The coarse woven wool of the plaid smelled musty, but it worked well as a makeshift towel. While he dried his hair and body, a small brown mouse scurried out from under the pallet. The little creature sniffed the air, eyed him, and promptly ran back under the bed.

"Mice in a mockup." Gavin slung the tartan over his shoulder and rubbed his eyes. "I'm thinking no."

He felt a painful gnawing in his gut, which he'd never suffered with his ALS, and then went still as he realized what it was: hunger. His disease had been slowly robbing him of his ability to swallow, giving every mouthful he took the potential to choke him to death. Depression and side effects from his medication had killed what was left of his appetite. Now he felt as if he could eat a deer from hoofs to antlers. Carefully he prodded his neck, and swallowed several times before he reached the only logical conclusion he could.

"I'm cured." His vision blurred for a moment, and he glanced up at the cobwebbed roof beams. "Sorry for calling you evil and old. Though you're still and will ever be a bastard."

A more thorough search of the lodge turned up a number of archaic but useful items: a bone-handled dirk, a half-empty sack of oats, some crockery, a jar of rendered animal fat, a bucket made of pitch-covered wood, and a stack of split, seasoned logs.

*If some poor student had tried living here as if it were the Dark Ages*, Gavin thought, *roughing it would have proven too much.*

He'd watched a few shows on the telly where people went back to living as if they were Edwardians and Victorians and such.

"I'd have tried my hand at being a highlander," Gavin muttered as he stacked firewood in the hearth. "They never took any shite from anyone."

He looked for matches and instead found a cracked leather pouch containing a grooved stone, a rusty curl of metal, and a wad of dried fungus. He'd started enough camp fires in the service to know a tinder kit when he found one. Dimly he remembered his sergeant bragging of starting a blaze with flint, and tested the metal and stone. A spark jumped from the rusty curl as he struck it against the groove in the stone. A few minutes later he'd built a respectable fire and used the caldron to heat water and oats into porridge.

While he waited for the oatmeal to cook Gavin rinsed the dusty crockery, and used the dirk to whittle one end of a kindling stick into a flat oval. In his mind he kept running through his spotty memories, hoping to recall something that would explain his situation. Nothing did. He'd watched Jema; the ground had shaken; he'd been blinded for a moment; the trench had collapsed under her just as he'd fallen in; and then he'd blacked out. That was all he had to go on.

The porridge turned out thick and lumpy, but he didn't wait for it to cool. Even as it scalded his tongue, the hot sticky oats tasted better than anything in his memory, and completely filled the hole in his gut.

Once he finished eating, Gavin draped the damp tartan over a chair by the fire, and then stepped outside to take a piss. Even that felt grand. From the lodge he spotted a trail leading up into the ridges. Now that the temperature was plunging, he retrieved the tartan before he followed it. The path wound through the woods until it slanted up to end at a high crag. When he walked to the very edge of the cliff, he finally saw what lay beyond the ridges.

A crooked valley spilled down to a river and a sprawling terrace of land covered in high, green grasses. Thousands of red deer moved in a single, enormous herd as they grazed peacefully across the glen. The river itself branched off into low, wide waterfalls that spilled into small, rocky lochs. To the west he could see a much larger body of water, and beyond that the ocean. Long dark shadows on the horizon formed the Black Cuillin mountains on the Isle of Skye, and more of the outer islands beyond that.

Gavin had lived in Scotland for most of his life. This was his world, but he no longer recognized it. Entire villages and farms were gone. He saw no ferries, telephone poles, cars or roads. Something more nagged at him, something huge, until he worked out what it was.

The Skye Crossing, the bridge that spanned Loch Alsh to connect the island to Eilean Bàn, no longer stretched over the water. Twenty-four hundred meters of bridge had vanished, as if it had never been built.

He went still as the only explanation for what he was seeing began to dawn.

"Because it *hasn't* been built," he murmured under his breath. "Not yet, anyway."

# Chapter Four

WAKING UP IN the arms of Tormod Liefson had made everything seem a little less terrible, at least until Jema's hands disappeared. She jerked them away from him, and when she looked down she couldn't see her abdomen or legs either. A scream rose in her throat as she flung her arms around his strong neck, but the sound died when she saw nothing where she felt his hair and skin against her forearms.

"Easy, lass," he said and clamped his long arms around her, holding her against his chest. "You're still with me. I can feel your shape and your heat."

"But I'm invisible," she whispered, her

throat so tight she felt as if she were strangling.

"Aye, you are." He rubbed his hand over the back of her head. "I ken you're afraid, but you neednae be. I'll no' leave you. Only look at me, and breathe, slow and deep."

She stared at his face as she gulped in more air. Everything about him seemed familiar, from the shaggy mane of bleached gold hair to the sunlit sea of his eyes. The torch's flickering flame made shadows dance across his features, masking him with a sterner expression than he'd had when she'd first seen him. As her heartbeat slowed, a cool sweat broke out over her skin. She felt the panic easing, and exhaled slowly. Her arms began to show in semi-transparent outlines, and then filled in and solidified, as did the rest of her body.

"Oh, thank god," she exhaled. She pulled his head down to hers, and pressed her wet cheek against his, sobbing with relief.

Tormod held her without speaking, his hands stroking her shoulders and back as he let her weep. She clung to him like the rock he had become to her. All she knew was this man, and this place. Finally she pulled back and wiped at her face with her shaking fingers.

"Am I still here?" She could see that she was, but she wanted to hear his voice again.

"You never left, lass." He removed his tartan and swaddled her with it. "I'm no' a healer, but I should see if you've other hurts."

"While you can still see me," she tacked on, and pressed a hand to her brow. "My head is pounding, but that's all." She saw his expression and nodded. "Of course, you should check me. I'm sorry, this is just unnerving."

"'Tis no' a picnic for either of us," Tormod said, and smiled a little. "At least, that's what my friend Red would say."

The gash on her head throbbed in time with her massive headache, but Tormod handled her carefully. With his hands he felt along her limbs, squeezing just enough to feel her bones before he flexed her elbows and knees. He also pressed his palm against her belly, and ran it from the bottom to the top of her spine. Finally, he used the torchlight to inspect her clothing for blood, but all that he found had come from her head wound.

"Don't do that," she said as he ripped off one sleeve from his tunic.

"I've naught else to bind that gash, and the smell of your blood will draw…trouble." He brushed her hair back and carefully wound the sleeve over the wound and around her head before knotting the ends. "We've a long trek back to where I left my mount. We'll try your legs now."

"You could leave me here." Though she hated the suggestion the moment she said it, leaving the only place she knew didn't seem right. From the way Tormod scowled he didn't like the idea any better. "Maybe my family lives nearby. They'll be looking for me, won't they?"

"You're no' from here, lass. There's more, and I'll tell you what I ken, but later. I must take you to…a safer place." He set his hands on her shoulders. "Can you make yourself unseen again? If you can will it, 'twould help when we need you no' to be noticed."

Just thinking about it made her stomach knot. What if she disappeared and didn't come back? Who could just disappear anyway? How in the world could she will such a thing? But as he waited, his kind eyes met hers.

"I wouldnae ask it of you," he said quietly, "if I didnae have to." He offered her an encouraging smile. "I'll be here."

She pulled in a long, slow breath through barely parted lips. For him she would try.

She closed her eyes, and recalled the awful fear and panic she'd felt the last time. When she looked down at herself, her body began turning transparent. A moment later she disappeared completely.

"Clever lass," Tormod said. "You've done it." He slid his hands up to cradle her face. "Now breathe, as before, and come back to me."

When she turned visible he smiled, and she felt a flicker of suspicion. "You know what this is? What's making me do this?"

"Mayhap," he said and released her. His expression sobered as he glanced at the horizon. "We must go. You need sheltering, and I'm to report for duty at dawn."

Holding up the torch to light the way, Tormod guided her out of the clearing and through the maze of close-planted oaks. "Tell me if you need a rest."

Her knees had felt a little rickety, but were growing steadier with every step. "Why did you ask if my name is Jema?"

"I thought I heard it, just before I found you." He took her arm as they encountered a fallen elder, and boosted her over it. "I've naught to call you but my lady and lass."

"Or the Disappearing Woman." She shuddered a little. "How is it possible that I can vanish at will?"

"Such things are gifted by the gods," Tormod said and stopped. He held the torch lower to the ground, and changed direction. "'Tis in your blood, my lady."

"Until I remember my name, I'd rather you call me Jema." She slid her hand down to his, feeling a little safer when his fingers twined with hers. "You're not Scottish, are you?"

He made a rude sound. "No' even a little."

Tormod fell silent as he retraced the path that had brought him to her, but Jema didn't mind. Nor did the long walk bother her, which meant she was in good physical shape, and knowing that pleased her. The only thing she hated was the huge black wall in her head preventing her from remembering who she was, how she got here, and why she felt so wretched each time she thought of that trench in the ground.

At last they emerged from the forest into a broad clearing, where Tormod extinguished his torch in the ground, and went over to an enormous white horse tethered to a bush.

"We'll ride from here." He removed the four-horned saddle, gave it a regretful look, and tucked it in the bushes. "'Twill be quick."

Jema didn't feel afraid of the horse, but when her rescuer removed his ripped tunic to fold it over the gelding's back she felt startled. Inked on his shoulder was a large symbol shaped vaguely like a ship's helm wheel.

"I've seen this symbol somewhere," she murmured. Her fingers tingled as she reached out to touch it, and then she felt something cool rush up the length of her arm. A fragment of memory flickered through her thoughts. "Are you a Viking?"

Tormod covered her fingers with his, closing his eyes before he removed her hand.

"Aye, and we'll talk on that later as well. We must ride now."

Jema guessed he didn't want to tell her too much, and that it had something to do with the differences between them. His garments appeared crudely-made, while hers seemed much more sophisticated and complicated. He wore fur and leather and linen, but her clothes had been made from different varieties of cotton.

"Where are you taking me?" she asked, and when he muttered something under his breath, she answered him in the same language. "Please, do not curse me. I'm only trying to fathom this."

Tormod jerked away from her as if she'd slapped him. "You're not druid kind." Before she could ask what he meant, he switched back to English. "You mustnae speak in our tongue to anyone but me, and only when we're alone."

She felt a small pang of hope. "You mean, I'm Viking, too?"

He started to speak, stopped, and then exhaled. "'Tis no' a language a Scotswoman would speak."

"Well, that's something, then." She looked past him to the road that had brought him here. "Can you take me to your tribe? Maybe one of them will recognize me."

"My tribe is gone. I was—I am—the last." He gripped her by the waist, and lifted her onto the horse before he swung up and settled behind her. As he gathered up the reins, he said, "Jema, do you ken what *huliðshjálmur* is?"

She knew the word translated to "the helm of hiding," but she didn't know how she knew that, or what the phrase meant. After his reaction to her speaking their tongue, she decided to keep her knowledge a secret.

"No, I'm sorry," she said. "Maybe I did, but I've forgotten."

Tormod said nothing more as he guided the gelding out to a dirt road flanked by old, deep ruts. From there he urged the horse into a quick trot, and tucked his arm loosely around Jema's waist.

The countryside they rode through seemed vaguely familiar, although she kept expecting to see lights and homes where there were only woods and fields. She squinted as she looked around, but the jolting motions of the horse's trot magnified her headache. As soon as they reached his destination she'd ask if she could rest for a few hours, but until then, she'd just have to put up with it.

"Lean back against me," Tormod told her, and when she did he tucked her head against his neck. "'Tis no' far now."

Her cheek warmed where it pressed against the top of his shoulder tattoo, and the hammering pain behind her eyes slowly eased. Jema finally relaxed, soaking up the warmth from his tough body, and growing so drowsy she nearly dozed off.

Tormod's arm tightened around her. "You cannae sleep yet, Jema lass. When we reach the castle, then I'll doctor your wound, and put you to bed."

"Will you sleep with me?" she asked without thinking.

"Since I've only one bed, I'll have to." He hesitated before he added, "Or I'll pile some furs on the floor."

"You needn't do that," she said and stopped, eyes wide.

What had she been saying? She took her head from his shoulder. She'd only just met this man—hadn't she? With an upward glance, she stole a look at his handsome face. It felt as if she knew him. More than that, it felt right to be in his arms. But if they knew each other, wouldn't he have said so? She frowned as the thought made her head ache again. With a sigh she settled her head back down and rubbed her cheek against his ink. Warmth spread into her temple sending the last tendril of pain dwindling away.

The cold air grew damp and salty, and when at last the road led to a coastal town, she felt as if she should recognize the small, shabby-looking cottages and buildings. When Tormod reined in the gelding by an old, dark barn, Jema eyed the weathered wooden sign sporting a primitive red cow, and saw it again in her head, only flatter and much older, with most of the paint gone.

"Is this where you work?" she asked Tormod as he dismounted.

"'Tis where I keep the nag." He lifted her from the gelding's back to the ground, and pulled his tartan up over her head. "Stay here."

Jema nodded, and watched him open the

doors and lead the horse inside. She wanted desperately to go after him, for her head had begun aching again the moment he'd released her. On some level she knew that couldn't be right, but being close to him had made her almost forget she had a head wound.

A querulous voice came from the stable as Tormod emerged. "'Tis the last time you drag me from my bed to stable that evil beast, Liefson."

Jema watched the Viking swing around and wait as an old man came out to confront him. The stable master wore a crudely-sewn tunic over trousers that had been mended so many times the patches were virtually all that held them together. Tormod handed him some coins, which the old man snatched and tested with his few remaining teeth.

"'Tis happy for you that I'm no' a hard sleeper." The old man turned to go back into the barn, and then caught sight of Jema. "Who's this? I've no stall for your *hora*, you randy bastart."

Tormod grabbed the old man by the tunic, hauling him off his feet and up to eye level. "I came alone this night, and you'll keep that privy of a mouth shuttered."

"Please, don't hurt him," Jema said and hurried over to the men. She touched Tormod's arm. To the old man she said, "The warrior protects me. I am lost and hurt." She pulled back the tartan so he could see her face, and then realized she'd spoken in the old language. "Oh, damn. Sorry."

The old man stared at her, and then he gave Tormod a clumsy clout on the head before he whispered furiously, "Dinnae waste your time with me, you great fool. See to this *kyn-ligr kona*. If the Scots find a shieldmaiden here–"

"I ken," Tormod said and lowered the man back to his feet. "Say naught of her to anyone."

Jema's exhaustion and weakness suddenly dragged at her like heavy chains, and the pounding in her head had returned. She swayed as she reached out to Tormod. "I might need that rest now."

Her vision blurred as he bent to swing her up in his arms, and then she blacked out.

But her sleep wasn't dreamless.

A large hand clamped over her nose and mouth, and then she swam. But it wasn't swimming exactly. It was like being propelled through a bubbling river. Her clothes grew heavy with the strange swimming and clung to her body. Her head gash went numb in the frigid water.

But finally the warmth and smell of a fire roused Jema, and she opened her eyes to see orange-gold flames in a small hearth a few yards away. She lay on a soft bed of furs, with more piled atop her. The ceiling, walls and floor of the narrow room were made of stone blocks, which should have made it cold, but the air felt slightly warm. Parchment scrolls lay in neat stacks on a wide table in the corner. A rack of swords and axes hung gleaming on the wall opposite the bed.

Jema peered at the wide-bladed swords. The plain bronze pommels had curved cross-guards, and the tips of the iron blades appeared rounded rather than pointed. She knew how heavy they were, and that distinctive cross-guards had been a hallmark of Pictish weapons. But how did she know that? Had she carried a sword like those belonging to the Viking? Why would Tormod have blades belonging to another, very different culture?

On the other side of the small room Tormod crouched bare-chested and barefoot as he took a leather vest and some fur-topped boots from an open trunk. He'd already changed into clean trousers, and when she looked down at herself she saw he'd dressed her in an old, soft linen shirt. She touched her head, and felt a new bandage covering her wound as well, but her hair felt damp.

Some or all of the dream had been real. Tormod had brought her here, to his safe place, by water—through water. She would soon have to start asking questions, but for now she was simply too tired. That and she trusted him. If the Viking had wanted to hurt her he would have done so in the forest.

"You're awake," he said standing and came over to the bed. "How fares the head?"

"Better," she said, only now realizing it was true. She eyed the tunic he held. "Are you going to work now?"

"Aye, there's no dodging it." He shrugged into the vest. "I'm on duty until nightfall, but

I'll look in on you when I can. You mustnae leave my chamber." She cocked her head at him, and he must have seen confusion on her face. "We're in the keep. I managed to smuggle you in." He smiled a little. "If there's one thing a map-maker knows, it's the lay of his own keep."

She glanced at the parchment scrolls, but her eyes drifted to the weapons. Dimly she recalled what the old man at the stable had said about her.

"Why don't you want anyone to see me?" she asked. "Is it because I'm a shieldmaiden, whatever that is?" She glanced at the swords and axes. "What did I do?"

"I cannae tell you, lass," Tormod said as he sat down beside her to tug on his boots. "You speak my language, but your accent is Scots. You wear the helm of hiding, but your garments come from another time. In your pocket I found this map disc." He placed a small circle of blackened silver etched with tiny lines in her palm. A small hole at the edge look weathered, as though a chain had once been there. "'Tis older than me, and that 'tis *very* old. I'm fashed by you, Jema, well and good."

So was she, Jema thought. "What is the helm of hiding?"

"This." He took her hand and brought her fingers up to her cheek, where she felt a silky, circular pattern of lines on her skin.

Stunned, she pressed her palm over it. "I forgot that I have a *tattoo* on my face?"

"'Twas no' made with ink. It cannae be seen." Tormod eased her hand away. "I but felt the marks when you pressed your cheek against me, on the ride from the forest. Such skinwork is powerful magic among the Viking. That you wear it may mean you are a shield-maiden—a female warrior—but you have no battle scars."

She resisted the urge to look under her own tunic. But at the thought that he would have seen all of her when he took off her clothes, her cheeks flushed with heat. He pointedly looked at the floor and cleared his throat.

She looked around the room again: the weapons, the décor, the gorgeous man who had rescued her. It was all happening too fast. She lay in a fur-covered bed in a castle, had a tattoo that couldn't be seen, and had gone invisible. Of all the things that she had to worry about, being seen by Tormod was not one of them.

"What if my memory doesn't come back?" she asked. "What if we never find out who I am?"

"Then you'll be the lass you are now, and make a new life." His gaze grew shuttered as he tucked her hand back under the furs. "'Tis all you can do when everything is stolen from you."

Tormod put a cup of water and a golden pear within her reach before he belted his tartan over his tunic. He took down an axe from the wall and tucked it in his belt. Then he took one of the swords.

"Sleep now, Jema. I'll come back in a few hours with a meal for you."

"Pizza, please," she said half-heartedly.

She rolled over so she wouldn't have to watch him go. When she heard the door open and close, she pressed her face into the furs. Breathing in his scent made her feel a little safer, but that wouldn't help. Turning her head, she stared at his weapons, and clutched the map disc tightly as she let her fear swell.

"Nothing to see here," she whispered, closing her eyes as her body faded away. "Nothing at all."

## Chapter Five

DEEP BELOW THE surface of the Isle of Staffa, Quintus Seneca walked through the main passage to his command center. The subterranean fortress, which his men had spent a year carving out of the island's basalt heart, had at last been completed to his satisfaction. No sunlight could penetrate the enormous lair, nor could the enemy easily find it. His troops had become accustomed to sailing at night on black ships to avoid detection. Once he replenished the Ninth Legion's ranks, he would continue his quest to end the Pritani curse that had transformed him and his men into undead blood-drinkers. He'd also destroy those responsible, the McDonnel Clan, once he found their hidden stronghold.

A blur of red and gray swirled around him and became his prefect, Fenella Ivar, who fell into step beside him. "Fair evening, my lord."

He didn't smell any blood on her breath. "You should have fed before reporting for duty. Remember that hunger makes you prone to agitation and aggression."

She eyed one of the smiling mortal thralls passing them. "Listening to them mewling about how they adore me drives me mad, but you forbid me to rip out their tongues."

"You're using the captives from the furthest islands?" he asked.

He had suggested to her that the captives who didn't speak her tongue would prove less irksome.

She nodded. "Of course."

Quintus had spent most of the last year personally training Fenella to serve as his second. During their last battle with the highlanders, she had kept him from sharing the fate of her predecessor, the Marquess of Ermindale. He owed his life to the first female member of the Ninth Legion. Her unwavering devotion to him proven, he had set about teaching her to control her vicious impulses, and use her ability to move at inhuman speeds for reasons other than murdering indiscriminately. As a prefect she already commanded the fear-laden respect of every man in the legion.

She also needed to look the part of a command officer, so Quintus had ordered their mortal thralls to make her a Roman uniform tailored to her voluptuous form. He also insisted she wear her fair hair braided and coiled like a crown atop her head. Although they were no longer lovers, she was his most trusted officer now. If he was king of the undead, then she was his queen.

Fenella reported on the latest arrival of replacement troops from their estate in the lowlands, where specially-trained centurions turned enslaved mortals into undead. Once made dependent on blood, the recruits learned to live and fight as Roman soldiers.

"We'll need more thralls for the newly turned," he said, "but have them procured from the western mainland. We've taken enough females from the outer islands." He stopped as he saw the eight men waiting in his great hall. All were former slaves turned by Ermindale. "What is this?"

"A scouting party just returned from the mountains. I sent them to look for caves and tunnels we might use as shelters for our raiders and patrols." Fenella gestured to the optio of the group, who stepped forward and sank down on one knee. He saluted her with an arm across his chest. To him she said, "Report."

"We found a cave system in the forested region, Prefect, which we mapped. It is large enough to shelter a cohort, but there are no mortal settlements within ten leagues." The optio offered her a scroll. "The scent of a wounded mortal led us to a protected burial site in the woods where we retrieved this."

Quintus eyed the strange satchel the optio presented to Fenella. "What happened to the mortal?"

The man grimaced. "The mortal escaped through a gap in the oaks. We tracked the scent to the perimeter road, Tribune, but there it disappeared."

Fenella scowled at him. "Do you claim

that the mortal stopped bleeding in the middle of a road?"

"I cannot say, Prefect." He looked down at his boots. "It was near dawn, and the men were close to frenzy. I took them back to the caves to feed on a poacher we found in the forest. I discovered the pack when I returned the next night to inspect the burial site."

Fenella took the pack over to a map table. She turned it around and over before she glanced at Quintus. "Shall I tear it open?"

"Patience, my dear." He inspected the long strips of tiny, interlocked metal teeth, and then tugged on the thin tags at the center of them until they began to part with a slithering sound.

Inside the satchel were books filled with hand-written notes, drawings so detailed they looked exactly like the objects they depicted, and pages of finely-printed, illustrated paper. Quintus also found several transparent bags with seamed closures, a set of miniature tools tucked and rolled in a cloth, and a cloth purse filled with printed cards and more paper.

"That will be all," he told the scouting

party's optio, who bowed and left with his troops.

The writing Quintus recognized as very similar to the English alphabet used in Britannia. Aside from a few unknown letters here and there, he could read most of what had been written in the books, including the numbers noted at the top corner of some of the pages. What riveted him was an intricate drawing of a large golden diamond, and the words written beneath it.

"Freyja's Eye," he read aloud. "Said to harness the power of the sun. Blamed for sinking a fleet of ships off the coast of Scotland in the second century."

"Who is Freyja?" Fenella asked, her eyes gleaming with interest. "And how does her eye sink a fleet?"

"Freyja is Norse, if I'm not mistaken," Quintus replied before closing the book and putting it back in the satchel. "I must examine these. Go and feed, and then come to my library."

Quintus had commissioned a large, ventilated chamber to house his collection of illuminated manuscripts, most of which his men acquired while raiding abbeys and monasteries. The deceased marquess had done a great deal to make the library an impressive, luxurious space, but since Ermindale's death Quintus had removed most of the unnecessary furnishings. A chair, a table and enough light to read by were all he truly needed for his work.

All of the manuscripts he kept had to do with the history of the Caledonians, and some of the primitive tribes that had occupied Scotland long before the formation of the clans. Of particular interest to him were the Pritani and the druids, and the legends about their magic practices. Quintus knew that the McDonnel Clan had once been Pritani, and had sacrificed themselves to protect the heretical druids, but he still had not learned why.

After unpacking the burial site satchel, Quintus stacked the hand-written books on one side of his table, and the loose pages on the other. From his own shelves he took down a copy of *Gylfaginning*, an Icelandic manuscript detailing Norse legends. In it he found no mention of the golden diamond, and only a few references to the goddess Freyja herself. From what he had already read Quintus had assumed that Freyja was just a Norse version of Venus, the goddess of love and, through her son, the mother of her people.

The chamber door opened and closed, and Fenella strode in with a tall, fair-haired male thrall in tow. "Kneel down before the tribune, and keep silent," she told the slave, who eagerly dropped and bowed his head. "Tribune, I believe I may be able to shed some light on Freyja's Eye." Quintus eyed the thrall, making Fenella's lips stretch into a wide and pointy grin. "Not only did I not rip out his tongue, but it appears to speak Norse."

Quintus handed her the notebook with the image of the diamond. As Fenella inspected it, the male lifted his head and gave Quintus a pleading look. The thrall could not utter a word unless given permission. The compulsion to obey in mortals enthralled by blood exchange had proven absolute.

"You may speak," Quintus told him.

"My people told stories about the Eye, Master," the slave said eagerly, his words heavily accented. "'Twas a gift from the goddess Freyja to her lover, a mighty Norse warrior. The Eye could stop the sunrise or sunset, and turn the light into terrible shooting fire. But Freyja's lover went mad with the power of it, and hid the Eye to keep the goddess from taking it back."

"I have no use for folk tales," Quintus said, and noticed Fenella staring at one of the other drawings. "What is it?"

She showed him the image, and pointed to the edge of the illustrated pit. "Look at the tree roots. Mayhap 'twas once an oak grove." She nodded at the satchel. "Did the owner of the satchel fall into this pit?"

In the past three females connected with the groves had helped the McDonnel Clan to deal crushing defeats to the Ninth Legion. "Where did the lover hide the gem?" Quintus asked the thrall. "In the forest?"

The slave's eyes filled with tears. "Forgive me, Master, but I dinnae ken."

"You did very well, lad," Fenella said and stroked the thrall's head as she would a dog. "Shall I open a vein for you, Tribune?"

Quintus studied the mortal's tear-streaked face. "No. I want this one kept alive. He may prove useful again. Take him back to the thrall barracks and bring another for us. And give me an hour before you do. I want to look through these texts."

Fenella bowed before she hauled the slave to his feet and marched him out of the library.

Sorting through the papers from the satchel, Quintus set aside anything that mentioned the golden diamond, until he found a notebook with sketches of other objects. Under a circle inscribed with runes he read: *Rare shamanic map disc from the first century. Found in warrior burial site in Sweden. Led to hoard of gold and silver artifacts. Saga detailing map disc leading to Freyja's Eye could be valid.*

What had the scout said? *The scent of a wounded mortal led us to a protected burial site in the woods.*

By the time Fenella returned with the thrall Quintus had read enough of the texts to confirm that the owner of the satchel had also been searching for the burial site and a map disc that would lead to the diamond. If Freyja's Eye existed, and held sway over the sun, he could use the gem to shroud the land in eternal night.

The Legion would have free reign.

"Take that scouting party back out to the burial site," Quintus told his prefect, and showed her the sketch of the map disc. "Search for this and bring it back to me."

"As you command, Tribune," Fenella said and pushed forward a plump, smiling female thrall and followed her until she pressed the mortal's warm body against Quintus's hard, cold flesh. She smiled at him, showing her gleaming fangs. "But first, let us feast."

## Chapter Six

TORMOD TOOK A moment to compose himself before he emerged from the guard tower to take his place on the curtain wall. Though he'd managed to smuggle Jema into the stronghold, and hide her in his quarters, he needed to think about how to protect her until she recovered, and her memory returned. What the Hel he was supposed to do with her, he didn't know. What he did know was that he possessed not a single drop of Pritani or druid blood. Vikings such as he could not activate the grove portals. Whatever had brought Jema to this time had been none of his doing.

Fergus Uthar gave him a sour look as he approached. "You're late, you lazy bawbag."

"Aye, just as you were that day week last you spent cuddling the kitchen maid past dark." He squinted as the sunlight blazed across Loch Sìorraidh, illuminating the surface like the rainbow path to Valhalla. As it should have been for him, after the Romans had murdered him, but instead he was dragged back to life by the facking magic folk. "Was I wanted?"

"Are you ever?" Fergus said and handed him a water skin and the short horn all guards carried to sound an alarm. "Last night the lieutenant also came asking for you. I told her you were hunting." He saw the way Tormod looked at him and shrugged. "You vanish on this day every year, and always come back surly and empty-handed."

One man in five among the McDonnels was an Uthar, and Tormod knew them to be just as vigilant as Neacal, their chieftain. "No need to keep watch over me, Fergus. I've proven my loyalty time and again."

"Aye, so much so that you're missed now when you go hunting." He casually cuffed his bicep. "Mayhap next year you should bring back a brace of rabbits. 'Twill make your tale seem more convincing. I'm to bed."

"My thanks," Tormod said and clasped Fergus's forearm briefly before he assumed his post.

The spot gave Tormod a wide view of the ridges surrounding the loch and the castle. The Black Cuillin mountains looked as formidable as the stronghold they concealed, and had hemmed his view of the world for as long as he could remember. At times he wondered if his immortality would have him outlasting Skye's slippery dark stone giants. Someday he might stand and watch the ridges crumble to dust.

He shouldn't have loved it as he did, but he'd run the length of this island as a boy, and had drawn its jagged contours in the rich garden soil that had served as his first parchment. He'd learned from his father to fish with a long hook, how to ride and even to hunt, although he'd always hated killing the shaggy-hided red deer that lived in the ridges. He much more preferred following the natural paths through the Cuillin, and drawing the trails on birch bark to help navigate them again.

Arn Liefson had never approved of his drawing and wandering, so Tormod had learned to behave as other boys. It helped when he grew as tall and brawny as his sire.

Here on Skye Thora too had been born, his tiny miracle of a sister. Tormod still remembered exactly how his mother had tugged his baby sister free of her own body before handing her to Arn for swaddling. That a bairn could be such a blood-streaked, red-faced screaming little demon had mesmerized Tormod. His parents had been in awe of their daughter as well, but that was due to the large, eye-shaped birthmark in the center of her brow.

The tribe's shaman, Eryk, had been called to examine Thora, whom he pronounced marked by the Gods. When the infant had been presented to the tribe's headman he knelt before her and pledged himself her servant. That had set the tone for the rest of Thora's pampered childhood.

*You must protect Thora with your life, my son.* His mother had told him that every time she left his sister with him to go and work in the fields with his father. *Never forget that the Gods have marked her for greatness.*

Tormod didn't mind looking after her once she learned to use the privy and feed herself. He carved wooden poppets and spinning tops for her play, and even fashioned a tiny sword for her to use in mock duels with him. She had a natural grace and quickness that earned him more than one bruise.

"Take me a-raiding, Brother," Thora would demand as she ran about the cottage waving her little wood blade. "I shall kill all the wicked Pritani that steal our cows."

Being Thora's brother only became a liability when the time came for Tormod to undergo his manhood trial. He worked hard to prepare to run the gauntlet and survive the tribe's three tests of strength, skill and endurance. Among his tribe the wounds inflicted by the rites of passage were revered, and the more a boy suffered, the greater warrior he was considered. The only disgrace came when a boy died of his injuries, which cast shame on his kin.

Tormod had survived with only a dislocated shoulder, but Arn had insisted he mark the wound with the *Ægishjálmr.*

*'Twill inspire paralyzing dread in your enemies, my son,* his father said, *while defeating the fears in your mind.*

He couldn't tell his father that he felt no fears. Arn would never have believed him. Nor could he admit to his desire to be an explorer instead of a warrior. Men of his tribe did not go raiding, but they fiercely defended their families and land. Tormod had no choice but to train as a warrior, and he specialized in the axe. But unlike many of the Vikings who took it up as a chopping and hacking weapon, Tormod had also learned how to throw it. He could easily hit the knot in a plank of wood at fifty paces.

Now, looking down as the clan's mortal servants began emerging from the stronghold, he imagined taking Jema back to her future, and staying there with her. He had traveled to her world once to save his best friend, so the marvels there would not be entirely baffling. If he could not keep her safe in his time, the only option might be to journey to hers.

But if she were better off there, then why

had she been sent back in time to him? What did the Gods expect him to do with her?

"I told you he'd be here," a low, somewhat annoyed female voice said from behind him.

As Evander Talorc and Diana Aber walked across the curtain wall toward him, he saluted the captain of the guard, and eyed his best friend. "Fair morning to you both."

"Viking," Evander said evenly. Tall, lanky and deceptively lean, the captain exuded a decidedly menacing aura. He was a vicious fighter, and his skill with a spear was unparalleled. Yet he had changed since returning to the clan's fold to take charge of the castle's guard. "You're late."

Tormod could tell tales as skillfully as a skald. But if he ended locked in the dungeon for lying, who would care for Jema? Better to admit than deny. "I was, Captain. Forgive me."

"Fergus told me you went hunting last night," Lieutenant Diana Aber put in. As tall as Evander, and possessing the same mane of gilded copper hair, the former San Diego police detective had become a gifted tracker. "Next time let me know. I'll come with."

"You despise hunting everything but the undead," Evander told her before he regarded Tormod. "Must I put you on until dawn tomorrow, Viking, to remind you of your duty?"

The thought of leaving Jema alone for two days made Tormod's blood curdle. Ducking his head, he said, "'Twillnae happen again, Captain. You've my word."

"See that it doesnae," Evander said and continued along the wall to the opposite tower.

The lieutenant leaned back against one of the wall's shield stones and folded her arms. "Pissing off Talorc, not very smart. He's creatively mean. Also, you hate hunting even more than me. What's going on with you?"

He considered lying to her, but Diana's former profession had trained her to detect such things. Confiding in her about Jema was also unwise.

"I did go hunting, but no' for game. I've been searching for my sister Thora's grave." He gestured toward the mainland. "She's buried somewhere in the highlands. I leave Skye this day each year to look for her."

Diana frowned. "Why not tell anyone?" Before he could answer she smacked her palm against her brow. "Because when you were all still mortal the Pritani burned your settlement and wiped out your tribe."

He shrugged. "'Tis long past and naught to us as we are now. I've no' held a grudge."

"Then you're a better man than me, pal." She bumped her shoulder against his. "You could have asked me to join the search. After all, it was my job as a cop to find the missing."

"She's no' missing, Red," he snapped. "She's bones." Tormod immediately regretted his tone, and added, "Dinnae make a destrier of a dormouse. 'Tis naught to do with the clan. 'Tis a private business—mine."

Diana regarded him in silence for so long he thought he might spill his spleen then and there. "Okay. If you change your mind, I'm happy to help. Next time you might also mention it to Evander, though, so he doesn't think you're catting around in the village."

"I never hunt village pussy," he assured her gravely, making her chuckle. "Why did you look for me last night? Never tell me Aber has stopped spotting you with your grain sack lifting."

"No, Raen is having the smith forge me some dumbbells. I'll explain when they're finished. I came looking for you because I need all the detailed maps you've got for the northern, eastern and western coasts." She tugged a scroll from her back pocket, opening it and flattening it on the top of the shield stone. "Another black ship was spotted by free traders running at night here, near the Isle of Mull. They drew me this gem as reference, which is basically useless."

Tormod scowled as he examined it. "You might use it to wipe an arse."

"Don't be snide, not everyone can cartograph like you." She pointed to a spot on the crude map. "We need to start searching the coves and inlets around here for a new undead lair. But if they're still using black ships they could be anywhere there's water deep enough to safely anchor. I'd like to organize a grid of all the possible locations based on your maps, which do *not* resemble kindergarten art."

He nodded. "I'll deliver them to your work room once I'm off duty tonight."

"You look exhausted, so tomorrow morning is fine." Diana crumpled the map and let it drop into the moat far below them. "Just don't be late for guard duty again or Evander might chuck you out a window."

❧

JEMA WOKE to the scent of cinnamon and honey, and the gentle touch of a callused hand on her brow. She opened one eye to see her Viking sitting beside her and smiled. "Did you bring me a pizza?"

"I dinnae ken what a pizza might be," Tormod said, and helped her sit up before he placed a tray on her lap. "I have cannel brew, oat cakes and pottage with leeks and chicken. If you're a good wench and eat the lot, I'll slaughter an ox for your evening meal."

His voice had a slight rasp to it and Jema realized why: he'd hadn't yet slept. Feeling horribly guilty, she set the tray aside and pushed away the furs.

"I'll eat while you take a nap," she said. "When do you have to go back on duty?"

"Now."

"*Now?*" she said, her voice as plaintive as she felt. "So soon?"

Quickly Tormod put a finger to her lips. "Shush now," he whispered and glanced at the door. "Someone may hear."

Jema stilled, only flicking her eyes to the door for a moment before the warmth on her lips drew her attention. Tormod stared at her mouth as though he felt the same thing. With a barely perceptible touch, he brushed his finger along her lower lip. But no sooner had he started than he yanked his hand away. He covered her legs with the furs and then shifted on the bed to keep her from rising.

"I'll have a look at your wound before I go."

She grimaced as he removed the bandage and inspected the gash, which to her felt hot and tight. "How bad is it? Do you think it'll infect?"

"'Tis closed already, so no' likely." Carefully he probed the area before taking her hand and bringing her fingers to the short, jagged seam across her temple. "You heal like the Eir-beloved."

Jema knew Eir, the goddess of healing. She was often invoked in kennings for women. Thinking of the Norse goddess made some of her tension ease. She might not know her own name, but everything she did understand made it clear that she had been born to the Viking.

"Maybe it wasn't so bad," she ventured.

His golden brows arched. "Do you wish to see how red you left your coat and semat? And they're no' soaked in bearberry juice."

"Head wounds always gush like fountains," Jema chided without thinking. "When I was a wee lass, I fell out of our old alder tree and split my scalp. I thought Mum would… faint." She stared at him. "Tormod, I have a mother."

"Aye, and a father. We all of us have." Tormod took from his belt a tiny carved box the size of a walnut. When he opened it a bitter-sweet scent tickled her nose. "'Tis a healing salve our people used to keep their wounds from festering. My mother made it of yarrow, wool fat and honey."

Jema held still as he carefully applied it, expecting a sting but feeling only an easing of the tightness. "Are you going to tell anyone about me being here?"

His mouth tightened as he drew back. "No' yet, lass. Mayhap once you've mended, and your memories come back."

"I don't want to get you into trouble." She reached out to touch his arm, and then saw the tattoo on his shoulder start a slow spin. Her head decided to do the same. "Are you sure I'm not feverish? Because if I'm not, your ink is moving."

He turned his head and dropped his chin to watch it. "Oh, fack me, *no*."

Jema took her hand away, and the ink went still again. When she reached to touch the tattoo directly, she felt something tugging at her fingertips, as if his skin were magnetic. The moment she made contact a bolt of strange, cool delight sizzled across her palm. The pleasure spread over her inner forearm, where it seemed to contract and form into a long, thin patch of ice. Despite the minor discomfort, she splayed her hand over his ink, and felt it slowly start spinning again.

"What is doing that?" she whispered, but when she looked into her Viking's eyes she saw their pale blue color had changed to something fierce and inexplicable, like ice on fire. "Tormod?"

"Dinnae move," he commanded. He dragged in some air, his broad chest expanding like a huge bellows. A long bead of sweat trickled down the side of his face. "It cannae be. I am no' one of them. 'Twas never my tribe."

Jema sensed he wasn't speaking to her, and whatever was happening to him was causing pain. But with that realization something strange rose up in her. As though in response to his words, it swept away her concern and replaced it with a sudden sensual curiosity.

"I think I'm your tribe," she said lowly.

He flinched. "No. Thora is gone and I've no' ever… No, lass, you cannae be."

"It doesn't matter," she said and stroked his tattoo. Then she pressed her other palm to his lean cheek. "Let me help you." She shifted closer, leaning into him as she slid her hand to the back of his neck. "Come here."

Resting her brow against his made him close his eyes, while a peculiar heat shimmered through her, intensifying her blooming desires.

"Jema," Tormod muttered, his whole body tense. "Clout me."

"Hmmm?"

Why was he talking? Jema wondered. They didn't need words. They didn't need anything but their hands and mouths and skin.

"I cannae stop if you dinnae." His hand pushed into her hair, and he tilted her head at a slight angle as he looked all over her face. "Gods, you're lovely."

Jema liked the way his fingers curled against her scalp. Everything inside her seemed to be turning to hot slush. "Maybe it's me, or something inside me." And she didn't care if it was. "Are you afraid?"

"Of you? Never." He cradled her jaw with his hand, and covered her lips with his.

Her Viking's scent enveloped Jema, wrapping her in delicious heat and spice, while his mouth fed the fire in her belly. He kissed her with such complete, shattering passion that at first it was all she could do to hold on and be open to him. Then the bold thrust of his tongue against hers seduced her, unleashing a shocking hunger for more. She tugged him down on top of her, clutching his vest when he tried to roll away. When his big hands clamped over her wrists she released a long, heartfelt moan.

"You're like rose petals," he muttered, taking his mouth away for a moment before ravishing her lips again.

Jema wanted to feel his skin, and hated the leather preventing her from touching it. She tore at his vest until he reached between them, opening the fasteners. He reached to her shirt and dragged it up, uncovering her breasts. Nothing felt as good as the ripped, unyielding hardness of his chest abrading her puckered nipples. The sensations that flooded her became so intense she arched up and cried out into his mouth.

A harsh knock sounded at the door.

Tormod clamped his hand over her lips as he lifted his head and turned it toward the door. "What is it?"

"You're wanted in the map room, Viking," a deep voice out in the corridor replied. "'Tis the laird waiting, so make haste."

Tormod waited until the sound of footsteps receded before he took his hand away from Jema's mouth. "Forgive me."

He sounded as stunned as she felt. As he sat up he covered her breasts with the shirt, then got to his feet. She watched him jerk off his torn vest and take another from his trunk. At least he was feeling as frustrated as she did, or she hoped he was. She lay on the bed not moving to cover herself with the furs.

"Is the laird as good as a clout?"

"Better," he said, pulling on the vest and fastening it quickly. "No, lass," he said as she started to rise. "If I kiss you again, I'll have you. I'll have you against the facking wall." When she swung one leg over the side of the bed he muffled a groan. "Jema, think. We ken naught of your life. You could belong to another man. You might have bairns–"

"No kids," she replied instinctively and pressed her hand against her abdomen. "I can't tell you how I know, but I'm not a mum." She splayed out her fingers. "No rings or ring marks. I don't think I belong to anyone."

*But you*, her heart added.

"We willnae be sure until you remember." He rubbed a hand over his face. "I cannae keep the laird waiting. I… Forgive me."

Tormod left, as did the last of the strange desire that had almost taken her over. Her body still throbbed, though sullenly now. The aching tightness of her beaded nipples made her press the heels of her hands against her eyes. When she rolled onto her side she felt the wetness between her legs. A tiny lump made her reach under her arm and pull out the map disc, which had gotten wedged in the linens.

She should have been grateful for the interruption, Jema thought as she idly rubbed the disc. Without that knock on the door she felt absolutely convinced she would have had sex with Tormod. But now she wanted to find the deep-voiced man and slap the sense out of him, and then hunt down her Viking.

Jema reached out to put the disc on the bed side table, and saw a mark on the inside of her forearm. She turned her arm toward the lamp, and saw the tattoo of a bright golden arrow on her skin.

Carefully she touched the ink. "How the hell's bells did you get there?"

## Chapter Seven

THANKFULLY THE LAIRD'S questions had been few. Diana had told him of the new map of coves and inlets and Lachlan had wanted to assure himself of the territories it covered, including the most likely places where the undead might hide. As the hour was late, the laird did not tarry, nor did Tormod.

He went directly to an unused guest room and stole the straw-stuffed mattress. He dragged it quickly through the empty hallways to his room. Without a word, he opened the door, pulled it in after him, and shut the door. Though he heard Jema stir, he didn't look at her as he crossed to the far side of the room and put down the mattress.

"You don't have to do that," she told him as he took a sheet and blanket from his chest. "I won't kiss you again, I promise."

"I cannae make the same vow, so I must."

He made the bed and stretched out on it, looking down to see his feet hanging over the end. He'd have to wear his boots or his toes would be frozen by morning. If only his cock would do the same, but no, he still felt as hard as Gramr, Sigurd's dragon-slaying sword.

"Don't you trust me anymore?" Jema asked, her tone woeful now.

If he comforted her he would have her, and then the Gods would surely stuff his shit of a soul up a dragon's arse.

"I might jar you in my sleep, lass. We dinnae want that gash to reopen."

"That's not what we want and you know it," she said, her voice sharp. "I'm sorry," she said quickly. "I didn't mean to say that." She thumped back on her pillows. "I've been staring at the map disc but can't make sense of it. I've tried to remember something—anything—about my life but all that does is make my head hurt." She blew out an exasperated sigh. "What's wrong with me?"

"Naught that I can tell you," he said, though he had his suspicions.

She could be possessed by one of the Pritani's war spirits. That a woman could be chosen by the Gods for such a thing didn't disturb him, but such a suggestion would outrage the clan. Among their tribes, only men had been offered to the spirits.

Tormod considered speaking with one of the druids that regularly attended the clan. Since learning that Diana belonged to his bloodline, Bhaltair Flen had become more approachable. The old druid certainly knew much about the Pritani. His acolyte ovate, Cailean Lusk, still remained in training, but something about him had always made Tormod suspect he was not as young or as inexperienced as he appeared.

Still, he didn't want to instill false hope, so he finally said, "We'll fathom it as we may, Jema."

When she didn't reply he sat up and saw that she lay curled up, her eyes closed. In slumber her beauty was ethereal, as if she hadn't a care in her heart. Silently he rose and walked over to snuff out the candle by the bed. As his eyes adjusted to the dark, he simply stood there to watch her sleep.

It occurred to him that he'd never brought a woman to his bed.

To see her pale locks spread over his pillow made him imagine waking to such a sight every dawn, as married men did. He knew himself capable of love. Thora and Red both owned bits of his heart, but he had never considered taking a wife. Even if it were not forbidden by the laird, what had he to offer as a husband? He had no tribe and no rank. Immortality had taken from him any hope of siring children. The clan regarded the maps he made as theirs. His weapons, some coin, a saddle and the gelding were all he truly possessed. Besides, any wife he took would age and die while he remained unchanged.

Tormod stared down at Jema. For the first time since his mortal death he realized he didn't want to spend eternity alone.

Dropping down on one knee, Tormod put his face as close to Jema's as he dared. She smelled of the herb poultice he'd used earlier on her wound, as well as her own soft sweetness. He inhaled and tasted the honey on her breath from the brew he'd made her, that and the dried mint sprig he'd given her to clean her teeth. Her lips parted as she murmured in her sleep, and he lightly traced her lower lip again with a fingertip. The delicate curve felt as thin and silken as a rose petal.

To do more would have woken her—and shamed him.

Summoning all his will, he slowly rose and returned to his short bed. With his arm under his head as a pillow, he watched her from across the room until he fell asleep.

The days that followed crept by on crippled, dragging hours for him. Most nights when he returned from guard duty Jema was awake, but he made sure to keep his distance once he brought her meal tray to her. For a woman accustomed to the countless comforts of a faraway future she never complained, although she insisted on bathing every day, and washing her bloodied garments so she might wear them again.

"You'll barely have a scar," he told her one night as he removed her head bandage to expose the now-healed gash. "And that your hair shall hide."

"I'd like to wash it if I could," she said, touching the strands around the wound, which were stiff with dried blood. "A bucket of water and a catch basin for rinsing should do."

He'd convinced Meg Talley, the clan's chatelaine, that his appetite had expanded enough for two, but like the other men he bathed in the loch.

"I've another idea," he said.

Few of the McDonnels ever went to the basement level of the stronghold, where the water heated by an underground thermal spring welled up into a series of enormous cisterns. One of them had once been used as a laundry before the clan built a proper wash house. Late that night he led Jema down a back passage to the pool.

"If we chance upon a clansman, you must disappear," he told her, particularly now that she was dressed in her own clothes.

"If we run into someone," she assured him, "I won't even have to try."

In the cistern, mineral deposits had darkened the old walls, and the water smelled faintly of iron, but Jema looked as happy as if Tormod had showered her with gold. With his help she lay on the surrounding deck, and dangled her head over the water.

Trying not to splash her, he wet and lathered her hair.

"That soap smells good," she said, her voice almost dreamy. "Like minty nuts."

"You've a good nose, lass. My tribe made soap from conkers, salt and mint leaf." He cupped his hand to begin rinsing her silken locks. "I still make it for myself. 'Tis no' as harsh as the clan's ash and lard soap."

"You'd make a very good housewife," Jema teased as he gently squeezed out the excess water. "And if you've ever a mind to give up guard duty, you'd make a brilliant hair dresser."

"'Twas ever my secret hope to become a lady's maid." He eased her up into a sitting position and held her propped against him while he used a length of linen to rub over her damp hair. "That, or an axe man. Heads are my passion. And you?"

"I dream about tossing mounds of dirt from a hole in the ground," Jema admitted, and glanced down at the words on her shirt. "Maybe I'm a ditch digger. Or a prospector."

She tilted her head back to look at him. "You don't think I'm a grave robber, do you?"

Guilt stabbed him in the gut. "No, lass. That would be me." He shifted back and stood, offering her his hand. "We should get back now."

"You said no one would come down here until morning," she reminded him as she rose, and then gave the steaming water a look of longing. "Would it be all right if I take a bath first? No one drinks this water, do they?"

"We've other wells for that," he said. He knew from how often Kinley and Red bathed that women of the future were obsessed with bathing. Yet the thought of being in the same place with Jema while she was naked sent a surge of hot blood to his groin. "I'll fetch fresh garments for you."

"These are clean. I'd just like a soak." She studied his face. "You don't have to stay. I'm not going to faint and drown. If anyone besides you comes in, I'll do my vanishing act."

"Keep to the steps," he told her, pointing to the stone shelves leading down into the pool. "I'll stand guard outside. Call to me when you're done."

Walking away from her made Tormod feel relieved, but as soon as he took position outside the entry he wanted to turn and watch her. No, he thought, what he really wanted was to bathe her himself, as he had washed her hair. He imagined running his hands over her, and then carrying her up to his bed. There he could dry every inch of her soft, pale skin, and stroke her, and hold her against his own bare flesh until she fell asleep in his arms.

*Dinnae be a fool.*

Tormod knew if he lay naked with Jema he would not hold her chastely at all. No, he would be atop her before she could blink. His cock swelled as he thought of surging into her softness, and stroking hard and deep until her pleasure gripped and milked him of his own. So he would again and again. If she grew tender, he would idle away the hours caressing her, sucking her breasts and tonguing her pearl.

The sound of a splash and a yelp echoed around him.

His erection abruptly withered, and he ran

into the cistern chamber to see Jema clinging to the pool's edge. "Are you hurt?"

"Not at all, but I used the soap." She nodded at the steps. "The stone is so slick I can't climb out."

Without thinking he reached down and snatched her from the water, lifting her out and setting her on her feet. She swayed against him, as if her knees were buckling, and then braced herself on his arms. That she stood all wet and rosy from the water made him stare for an instant before he forced his gaze up and away from her.

"You don't have to stare over my head," Jema chided. "You've already seen me skuddie. I've no surprises for you."

"Just the same," he said tightly. He kept a hand on her as he reached down for the garments she'd left folded beside the pool, and put them in her grasp. That was when he saw something golden inked on her skin. "What's this?"

"It showed up after we…the first night I spent here." She extended her forearm to show him the golden arrow. "I don't know what it means. You didn't mark me before I woke up, did you?"

"No, lass. Without your blessing I'd never dare."

Instinctively, he reached out and touched the arrow. But the moment he made contact, it vanished. A piercing sensation on his shoulder made him look at his own ink. The arrow now occupied the center of his helm, and was pointing east. When he turned he saw the ink pointer adjusting to his change in stance to keep its direction.

Tormod was thunderstruck. She had marked him, just as a Pritani warrior would. But she was a woman, and from the future, where such things never happened. An ugly suspicion crept into his mind.

"Do you mean to own me?" he demanded. "Is that why you brand me now? Do you think I serve you, like some half-witted lout?"

Her eyes widened, and she turned as white as sea-bleached shell.

"No, I didn't do that. I mean, I never meant to do anything. I'm sorry." Jema began jerking on her garments. "I'll go back to the forest. There must be something there to explain the things I can do. I'll find a way to fix it." Her chin trembled as she looked at him. "Please don't be angry. You mean the world to me."

He knew that to be true but only because she couldn't remember anyone else in it. Remorse filled his suddenly heavy chest.

"I'm already ever your slave," he said, softening his voice, "and you're too jeeked to go anywhere but bed." He tugged her close, and rubbed his cheek against the top of her head. "I'm an ass. 'Tis naught but ink. 'Twill no' kill me."

"You should have left me there," Jema said and leaned her trembling body against him.

"Nonsense," he said into her hair, inwardly kicking himself for the way he'd made her feel. "We will go back to my chambers."

He held her against his side as they made their way out of the cistern chamber and ascended the back stairway into the guard tower. Once inside his room, she leaned back against him.

"I'm pure done in," she whispered, her eyes closing.

As she went limp Tormod swung her up

against his chest and put her to bed, covering her with his tartan. She tucked one hand under her cheek before she fell fast into a deep sleep.

Tormod believed she hadn't intended to mark him. Such a look of horror could not be feigned. It could have been a trick played by the Gods, to give his brains a stir. They enjoyed such torments. Or Jema had Pritani *and* Viking blood, which may have given her powers no one could fathom. If she didn't understand what the inking meant, he did.

He had been chosen as Jema's mate.

❧

JEMA OPENED her eyes to see moonlight filling the chamber, but no sign of Tormod. Her hair still felt damp, and when she got to her feet none of the weakness she'd felt after bathing returned. She must have fainted after the bizarre ink transfer that had made him so furious.

Her stomach knotted.

Had she hurt him? Had she violated some

sort of taboo? Or was it just another thing the Viking was hiding from her?

She remembered the look on his face. It had been one of shock, yes, but also recognition. What else did he know? Did the tattoo have something to do with the loss of her memory? Why couldn't she remember her life? How was she able to become invisible?

"What happened to me?" she said to the empty room, throwing her hands in the air.

All she had was questions.

Without thinking she turned to the door—but stopped. With every passing day since that first night in the forest, she'd felt ever stronger. Though she seemed to be able to control the invisibility, she had never really been put to the test. As she glared at the wood door, she took a deep breath and slowly exhaled. Tormod cared for her in a way that she felt deep in her soul. She had no doubt of his feelings. But his chamber had become her world. It was time to change that and find some answers.

He'd been working in the map room on some project for the laird all week, so he probably wouldn't be back for hours. He had, however, told her how to get to the room if she were in trouble.

This most definitely qualified.

Jema took off her socks, not wanting to slip, and grimaced at the touch of the stone floor on her soles. The unexpected cold jolted her into the moment. It took little to channel her power, since she was already afraid. As she reached for the door, her hand was already invisible, followed by the rest of her body. Carefully she eased open the massive door, but just an inch to peer outside. There was no one in the outer hall, so she slipped out and started for the stair.

In order to reach the map room, she knew she needed to leave the guard tower and enter the gallery above the great hall. But even as she approached, she was shocked by the din of dozens of voices. As she peeked over the low wall to the men below, she froze. The sight of so many large, well-built men drinking, gaming and arm-wrestling made her gulp.

If the McDonnels found that she'd been secretly living in the castle, would they make her a servant, or a slave? She had no defenses, just the ability to disappear. If they locked her in a cell, it wouldn't make any difference. They could do whatever they wanted to her, seen or unseen. No wonder Tormod had been trying to keep her out of sight.

She crept along the upper floor, until she realized their noisy conversations would mask any sound she made. She hurried toward the archway leading to the map room—and came to a sudden, stumbling halt. As two men walked out onto the upper floor, she nearly collided with them.

*Oh God, oh God, damn, damn—*

"Something is amiss," the tall, lanky man with a hard, attractive face said. He stopped barely a few inches from Jema as he looked down on the men. "He's hardly left his chamber all the week, and he's as silent as a wraith. Thrice I had to order him this morning to attend the laird before he heard me. What does Diana say?"

The man-mountain with him sighed and rubbed a hand over the jags of ink marking his face. "Naught to me, but you ken how she is with him. The shifty bastart never had such a mother. He seems distracted. I'll have a word."

The other man grunted, and they continued on.

Jema released the breath she'd been holding, and felt as if she might deflate and collapse. Pressing her hand to her fluttering heart, she forced herself to calmness. With conscious intent, she walked more sedately through the archway. More than once as other clansmen passed her she had to hug the wall, but finally she made it to the map room, which she knew because the door stood open.

Tormod stood in front of a large, whitewashed wall on which a huge map had been drawn in charcoal. From the way he looked from it to the map disc in his palm, he was comparing the two.

Jema strode in, pushing the door closed behind her. As Tormod swung toward her she rematerialized and said, "Just me."

"Jema, what do you here?" He hurried to her, looking all over her. "Are you hurt? Did someone find you?"

"I'm fine, no one saw me, and we need to talk." Deliberately she stepped away from him and made a circuit of the room. The shelves of neatly-stacked scrolls intrigued her as much as the giant map of Scotland he'd drawn on the white wall. "I need you to be honest with me, Tormod."

His jaw tightened. "I've no' lied to you."

"Yes, but you're keeping things from me." Jema picked up a fragment of shale, on which tiny triangles and swirls depicted mountains and rivers. "I can see it in your eyes every time we talk about the forest, or where I'm from, or who I might be. Tonight I saw it after the ink on my arm jumped to yours." She put down the shard and faced him. "What did I do to you? What aren't you telling me?"

"I dinnae say, for I dinnae ken for certain." The Viking dragged a hand through his hair. "All that you are has me fashed. You're this and that, and neither and both. There's no one to ask without revealing you're here. And what if I tell you wrong?"

"What if it helps me remember?" she countered.

"Tormod?"

The strange woman's voice made Jema dash back to the shelves, ducking behind them as she transformed. From there she watched as a tall, beautiful redhead and the man mountain she had encountered on the gallery entered.

"Who are you talking to?" the woman demanded.

"Myself, Red," Tormod said as he stepped between her and Jema, who looked down to see her body finish its vanishing act. "Raen," he said, nodding toward the big man. "How may I serve?"

"Raen is worried about you," the redhead told him flatly. "I'm not, because I'm used to your crap, but you have been acting a little weird, even for you. Oh, and Evander's highly annoyed with you, never a good thing with all these spears around the castle. So." She made a beckoning gesture. "Spill it."

Jema knew he wouldn't tell them about her, but she still measured the distance to the door. She'd have to move between the couple to get out of the chamber, and even if she remained invisible, they might feel her passing. She'd also be tempted to give the supermodel redhead a good, hard shove into something.

"I may leave Dun Aran," Tormod said abruptly. "'Tis safe to journey to Norrvegr now, and I wouldnae be noticed there as I am here. There is always work for a strong man who can hold his tongue."

"Sure, you'd be great, until they notice you aren't getting any older," the redhead drawled as she picked up the map disc he'd left on the table. She turned to the big man. "They burn witches in Norway, too, don't they, honey?"

"Aye, my heart," he replied. "Since the great freeze began, hundreds." His expression filled with contempt. "So you're done with us at last, Viking. You might have said. I'll be in the armory, Diana."

Jema flinched as Raen slammed the door on his way out, hard enough to make the wood panels crack.

"And now you've pissed off my husband, who no one but an army of undead can even knock over," Diana told Tormod. She came to stand beside him and looked at the wall map. "Here's what I *do* know. Rachel told me every time you see her you turn and go the other way. Lachlan is worried you're depressed and might try death by legion. Oh, and Meg thinks you're pregnant. What is this, the thing with your sister?"

"Aye," he snapped. "All my life is about

Thora, and finding her grave, and burying her on this facking island."

"So that's a no." She gave him a sideways glance. "I'm your best friend. I'll do just about anything for you. I'll even help you pack your shit. You really want to go?"

Tormod's mouth twisted. "I dinnae ken. No' yet."

Diana nodded. "Then get it together, pal, before the menfolk decide to beat the crap out of you just for sport. And I'm so pissed I might let them." She tossed the map disc to him, swatted his arm, and left the chamber.

Once the damaged door had creaked shut, Jema rematerialized and stepped out from behind the shelves. "An army of undead? Death by legion? Until they notice *you aren't getting any older*?"

Tormod went past her to bolt the door, and then took a dark bottle out from behind a stack of scrolls. He brought it over to the work table, where he sat down and gestured for her to take the chair next to him. As she did he uncorked the bottle, drank from it, and sighed.

"I ken you are no' from my time. Your garments, the way you speak, 'tis from the future," Tormod said. "Here oak groves may be used to move through time. Three other women like you have journeyed here from the future. Red is one of them. But only magic folk, druid kind, may do such things."

He told her of the laird's wife, Kinley, a wounded soldier and first to come back from the future. Diana had been the police detective assigned to find her. The latest arrival, Rachel, her husband had tried to murder her in their time before Evander found her in his.

"You think I'm from the twenty-first century," Jema said. Oddly that didn't make her feel alarmed, any more than it did to hear that oak groves worked as time-travel devices. However, it didn't explain why everything here felt so familiar. "If I'm like these other women, then why didn't you tell me?"

"Moving through the portal healed all of their wounds, but no' yours. They say they are Americans from a place called San Diego, and speak with the same accent. You sound like a Scot. 'Tis known that they have druid blood, but you've the look of a Norsewoman, and you speak my tongue. Some Viking have magic, but they cannae use the groves." He offered her the bottle. "You can."

"Losh," Jema said and took a sip. She let the fiery burn of the liquor blaze its way to her belly. "No wonder you kept quiet. I'm nothing but a great fankle." She met his gaze. "What about the other things Diana said? Was she joking?"

"Do you wish me to lie to you?" When she shook her head he took the bottle from her. "Then I cannae tell you."

She watched him drink. "So how do we unravel me?"

He moved his shoulders. "If you fell wounded into the portal in your time, it would have sensed your druid blood and brought you here. Or mayhap you were pushed. Rachel's husband sent her here by stabbing her in the back and burying her alive in a grove."

"That poor woman," Jema whispered and shuddered. "But I was still wounded when I arrived."

"Aye." His gaze shifted to the scar on her head as he turned the map disc in his fingers. "'Tis another shard of you I cannae make fit."

Then he lifted the disc. "And this too, the one thing that came with you."

Jema focused inward, trying desperately to remember anything from the black void of time before she landed in her Viking's arms. All that did was make her head start to pound.

"Tormod, somehow the pieces have to fit. But how do we figure it out?"

He shook his head. "'Tis only one way I can think of." He paused and took a swallow of whiskey from the bottle. "'Twill be others in the future who know you. Your family. Those who love you." He paused at those last words before plunging on. "We'll ride back to the forest tomorrow night. You can use the portal to return to your time."

"You want to send me *back*?" She stood so quickly she knocked over the chair. "I can't remember the future. I won't know anyone."

Tormod looked away from her. "'Tis your place in the world, Jema. Your home."

"No. This is home. The only home I know." She moved so that he had to look at her. "To send me back without my memories is the same as shoving me into a bottomless abyss. How could you do that to me? You *saved* me."

"I cannae keep you safe here at Dun Aran," he told her as he stood to loom over her. "Even with your powers, in time you'll be found. I dinnae ken what the laird would do with you. I ken what he will do to me for harboring an outsider."

"Then take me to a place where I *can* live, Viking. Because I'm not leaving."

# Chapter Eight

AS THE BRILLIANT orb of the sun dipped below the horizon, Gavin set the last of his snares near a patch of wild berries, and then shouldered his pack. Being restored to the big, brawny body he'd had during his service days would never pall. With every day that passed it was becoming harder to remember how weak he'd been. Back then even the simplest physical task had been almost impossible for him.

"A gastronomy tube will help you with the malnutrition and weight loss," his doctor had told him at his check-up last month. "You'll have to have one when you go on the vent, so to manage it now would be best."

The thought of tubes feeding him and

machines breathing for him while he lay help-less in a hospital bed had sickened Gavin. After that appointment he'd begun making plans, plans he no longer had to think about.

In this place, all that mattered was survival.

Since he had only himself to rely on he'd quickly taken stock of his situation. He had shelter, water and fire, but the provisions he'd found in the lodge wouldn't last forever.

The survival training he'd been given in the military served him well. To augment his food supplies he'd turned to trapping. Rather than waste his resources trying to take down big game like the local ghost-faced red deer, he tracked smaller ground dwellers. Once he had identified the tracks of rabbit, quail and grouse, and sorted out their runs and move-ment patterns, he went to work.

The simple snares he set had been used by hunters for millennia, and consisted of a small loop of baited, slip-knotted cord tied to a bent sapling. The other end of the loop he slipped over two twigs precariously hooked together, with the lower twig serving as a holding stake. When the animals went for the bait, they knocked apart the twigs, which released the tension on the loop. The energy provided by the sapling righting itself and the weight of the animal's body finished the work.

Successful trapping depended on numbers. He knew the more snares he set, the better his chances were at catching something. But game had proven so plentiful that he would soon have to think about curing the excess. That gave him a little reassurance as well. If he couldn't go back to his world, at least he wouldn't starve to death in this one.

Although he spent a good portion of every day looking after himself, Gavin hadn't given up his search for his sister. For his first days in this strange version of Scotland he'd used the river as his guide through the forest as he looked for Jema. Now he had marked or memorized enough landmarks and trails to navigate his way for miles in any direction. Yet no matter how many hours he spent sweeping the territory, he still hadn't found a single trace of his sister.

"She's here," he muttered to himself as he picked up his pace. "Even if I can't feel her, I'd know if she was dead."

Gavin had always shared a strong bond with his twin. From childhood they had shared some eerie connections to each other. He'd always been affected by her emotions. Even at a distance, whenever she'd hurt herself he would feel sick to his stomach. When she wept his own heart would throb with pain. Jema in turn had been tuned into his thoughts rather than his emotions. She always seemed to know what he was thinking or intending to say. She finished his sentences for him.

It infuriated him that they would both land in this place only to be immediately separated. Jema lived in her own world so much that she barely paid attention to her surroundings, but she would never have willingly left him to fend for himself. Could she have been arrested or abducted? Was that why she hadn't found her way back to him? And why couldn't he feel what she was feeling anymore?

Not knowing, and yet sensing she was alive, was slowly driving him mad.

Once he cleared the trees Gavin broke into a run. He'd never been fast but in his prime he'd been able to cover fifteen miles without stopping. Now he felt even stronger, as if he could manage twenty or thirty. That also made no sense to him. Why weren't his muscles still atrophied from the ALS? It felt as if he'd never been ill a day in his life. He sometimes still wondered if he'd died at the dig. It would explain why his connection to Jema felt so distant. Maybe she had survived.

Gavin ran alongside the river bank, knowing he was wasting time and energy but not caring in the slightest. Pitting himself against the uneven ground kept him from dwelling on all the unanswerable questions. It took another mile before he worked out enough of his anger to stop for a drink.

At the edge of the river he knelt down to scoop up a handful of the icy water. He'd never get tired of the crisp taste of it. Everything here was so pure and unadulterated it felt almost too good to be true—like his physical condition and his new life. Maybe he really was dead.

"No, leave me be," a woman's voice cried out in terror, making Gavin stiffen.

He took the dirk from his belt and moved silently toward the sobbing sounds she was making now. He crouched down enough for the brush to provide him cover, then parted a couple of branches and peered through.

Gavin counted five men surrounding her. All dressed in Roman soldier costumes but with very lethal-looking swords in their hands. The young victim wore a shabby gown that had been slashed open in the front, exposing the full curves of her white breasts. From the soaked condition of her dress and the dripping tangle of her hair she must have been bathing, or had fallen in the river. The men were grinning, showing canines filed to look like fangs, and jabbed their blades at her each time she tried to slip out of the circle or tried to cover herself with her hands.

"Please, spare me," the woman begged. "My da has been sickly, and I'm all he has. If I dinnae return home tonight he'll starve."

"We shall leave your corpse at his door for him to cook," one of the men jeered. "After we take your blood and your cunt."

Gavin's rage swelled—and his body soaked up the colors and textures around him. His mind flashed back to that moment in the forest when he'd backed against the oak in fury. He looked at his hands now, barely able to see them against the brush.

"No!" the woman cried out cowering away as one of the soldiers raised his sword high in the air.

Though Gavin didn't know what had happened to his body, it had provided him with the perfect camouflage. He saw his opportunity and sprinted from the brush.

The Romans didn't react as he ran toward the woman. He seized her in his arms and held her against his chest as he jumped from boulder to boulder over the river. He darted through the trees, not stopping until he was well out of sight.

The woman clung to him tightly, hanging on even when he set her on her feet. "Please, marster, dinnae kill me."

"I'm not going to hurt you," he said.

But when she stared up at him he realized he was still in camouflage. Again Gavin thought of that first time. His fear of seeing his hands turned to bark had cut through his rage and ended the spell. He pushed back his anger, now that the woman was safe, and was rewarded with the return of his own body.

"My name is Gavin McShane. You're safe with me."

"I but needed white willow bark," she said and tried to pull together the edges of her bodice, though her hands shook badly. "I lied to them. My da died last winter of plague. I'm the sickly one now. I'm so cold…" Her eyelids fluttered as she swayed and then collapsed.

Gavin caught her before she hit the ground, and the feel of her chilled flesh made him head directly for the lodge. Once inside he put her on the bed and heaped blankets over her before he built up the fire he'd left banked in the hearth. He filled a cup from the jug he used for drinking water and brought it over to the woman, who was watching him. Her pupils had dilated so much that her eyes appeared to be solid black.

He sat down beside her, helping her to sit up before he offered her the cup. "Drink a little. It will help you feel better. What's your name?"

"Fenella Ivar," she said and sounded calmer, though she looked at him with visible curiosity. "You are no' a highlander."

"Only in my dreams," he said and tried to

dry her hair with the end of a blanket. "Were you trying to cool down your fever? Is that why you went for a bathe?"

"The undead pushed me in," she said idly as she walked her white fingers up his chest. "You're no' afraid of the blood-drinkers, Gavin?"

"Do you mean the men who attacked you?" When she nodded, Gavin felt even more confused. "They actually meant to drink your blood?"

"No' mine, lad," she chided as she knocked the cup from his hand, and dragged him down on top of her. "I promised them yours."

Gavin couldn't believe how strong she was, and how quickly she put him on his back and straddled him. Then she struck his neck like a snake, biting into his flesh deep enough to draw blood, which she then began to suck. He shoved at her with all his new strength and sent her over the side of the bed.

Fenella was on her feet a moment later. "You're a brave one, lad. Your blood runs as hot and strong as your temper, I reckon." She laughed, flashing her bloody fangs.

"What the fuck is this?" he demanded.

"A well-laid trap. We've been watching you for nights and nights." She brought her thumb up to her blood-stained lips, and bit into her own flesh before she jumped on top of him again. "And now you'll be mine forever."

"Get off," he yelled.

He struggled to hold her at arm's length, but she didn't try to bite him again. Instead she pressed her bleeding thumb against his neck. Freezing pain jabbed into the twin wounds she'd left, and began shooting through him as if he were being riddled with bullets made of ice.

"What…did you…why?" he grated through clenched teeth as he convulsed.

"'Tis a kindness. The men cannae use you now. You belong to me." She caressed his cheek as gently as a lover, and crooned, "Dinnae fight. Aye, that's a good lad. Let it have you. You'll make a fine thrall."

The lodge went blurry around them, and Gavin felt as if his blood had turned to snow in his veins. As the shakes eased away, a new heat flooded through him. The heat of wanting. He looked at Fenella, beautiful Fenella who smiled back at him so tenderly he groaned.

"My god, did I hurt you?" he gasped.

He looked all over her, but he couldn't see any wounds. Even the gash in her thumb where she had bitten herself had vanished. He brought her hand to his lips to kiss the spot, and felt pleasure sweep away the last of the agonizing frost in his veins.

Everything in his life had been preparing him for this, for becoming hers. She made the world around them gray and cloudy until the only color he could see was the gold of her corn silk hair, the snowy perfection of her flawless skin, and the midnight sky of her black eyes.

Fenella Ivar was a goddess.

"You serve the glorious Ninth Legion now, Gavin," she said, sitting back on his thighs. "They are immortal Romans, and very powerful creatures. If you obey me in all things, I will give you the gift of eternal life."

"I want only you," he breathed.

Unable to control his passion another moment, Gavin rolled with her, pinning her under the bulk of his big body as he covered her mouth with his. He didn't care that she tasted of his blood. Kissing her was everything, the only thing. But her stillness made him lift his head to gaze into her shocked eyes.

"You have no fear of me," she murmured, and slid her hand between them to palm the thick ridge of his erection.

"Why should I be afraid?" Gavin said and shuddered at her touch. He fought to keep from ejaculating in his pants like some keelie tosser. "I adore you, Fenella."

"Aye, for you are my slave now." She moved her fingers to squeeze his balls. "You shall call me 'Mistress'."

"Keep playing with me and I'll be useless to you." He could hear the growl of impatience in his voice, but from the way she smiled she liked that. "Don't make me spend yet. I want to slide inside you, and pump you slowly until you come a dozen times. Let me have you, Mistress. You can't imagine how good I can make you feel."

The door to the lodge opened, and Gavin rose on his knees to see the five Romans from the river barging in. When he reached for his dirk, Fenella touched his wrist.

"These Romans serve me," she told him before she wriggled out from under him and climbed off the bed. "Put down your weapons. I have enthralled him."

It took Gavin only two heartbeats to put himself between Fenella and the men. "Get the fuck out."

"He does not seem to be completely under your control, Prefect." That came from the Roman who had jeered at Fenella at the river. "Perhaps you gave him too much of your blood, or you are too weak to compel such an ox."

The insult to his lady sent cold, killing rage pouring through Gavin, and for a second he thought he might literally explode. Then he was on top of the Roman, punching him over and over until the four other men dragged him off. He flung them away and went to finish killing the insolent bastard, when Fenella blocked his path.

She looked up at him, her lovely face stern now. "Gavin, give me your blade."

He drew the dirk from his belt, gripping the horn hilt tightly. "You said I belong to you now. I have to protect you, Mistress."

"Aye, you do, when I command it. But I am no' defenseless, my lad."

Fenella extended her hand, and when he reluctantly placed the knife in her palm she disappeared in a flurry of movement. She reappeared behind the Roman who had jeered at her, and drove Gavin's dirk into his neck. With one jerk of her hand she cut his throat.

The man's eyes widened as he uttered a choked cry. His faced turned gray and began to dissolve as if it were made of soft dirt.

Gavin felt only satisfaction as he watched the Roman collapse into a heap of ash, and the other men back away from Fenella. He came to stand beside her and studied the faces of the remaining Romans.

"They envy you for the way you move," Gavin said. "You're like the moonlight."

"They fear me for it," she corrected him. To the men she said, "Assemble outside and wait."

Once they were alone, Gavin tried to take her into his arms. Fenella placed her hand on his chest, and gently pushed him back.

"Pleasure later, my lad." She slid her hand up to his face. "We've work now."

He covered her fingers with his, reveling in the cool touch of her hand on his heated face. He frowned as she withdrew it. "What could be more important than pleasuring you, Mistress?"

"For this night, digging for treasure in a dead Viking's grave." She nodded toward the long-handled spade propped by the hearth. "You'll want that."

## Chapter Nine

TORMOD GAVE JEMA a scarf and long cloak to wear over the maid's kirtle he'd filched for her, and placed a basket on her arm. "You'll need to cloak yourself until we've reached the glen," he told her as he shouldered his own satchel. "None must see you leaving the stronghold."

"Then no one will." She closed her eyes and vanished.

He took down a torch to light the way as he guided her from his chamber and through the hidden passage outside. When he saw that the first pale streaks of dawn had already appeared on the horizon he extinguished the torch in an open water barrel, and took her to the post where earlier he'd tethered his mount, a large black mare sturdy enough to carry them both.

"I don't cast a shadow when I'm invisible," Jema's voice said right next to his shoulder. "How interesting."

"Or you do, and 'tis invisible as well." He inspected the stretch of ground they would have to cross before they reached the trail through the ridge. He mounted the horse, glanced about and held out his hands. "Take hold."

"I could walk beside you," she suggested.

"Aye, just as you might slide off a slope and break your lovely neck before I can catch you." He felt her grasp him and swung her up to settle behind him. "If anyone crosses our path, press yourself against my back and stay quiet. Remain thus until we are clear of them." When she grumbled something he added, "If you're unwilling, we can return to my chamber and sit there for twoday. I'll no' have to report for duty until sunset on the morrow."

"Yes, all right, I'm willing." She sounded resigned now. "Where are you taking me?"

"You wished to see where you might live if you stay. It is there we go now." He glanced either way before he started for the trail entrance.

Halfway to the trail Jema said, "Wait a minute."

He felt her turning back toward the stronghold, and wheeled the mare around. "'Tis what you wanted, lass."

"No, I mean give me a minute." Her voice sounded softer now. "Gods, Viking. You live in a castle hidden in a volcanic crater."

"Aye." Belatedly he recalled she had never yet seen the outside of Dun Aran. "'Twas built here to keep our enemies from finding us again."

She made a hmming sound. "Your ancestors were clever men, and very talented builders. Using the native stone as camouflage was ingenious. Even from this close it looks like part of the mountains."

"Quarrying the rock 'twas a monstrous task, and the hauling it up the slopes was–" He stopped, silently cursing himself for nearly revealing his immortal nature. "Such work."

"It's very old. Over a thousand years, I

imagine." She sighed. "Promise you'll give me a tour of it one night before you kick me out."

"I dinnae kick wenches, no matter how oft I am tempted." He touched his heels to the mare's side, and turned her back toward the trail.

Reaching the village required riding down to the glen, where Tormod had to stop again so Jema could admire the fairy pool and the old stone bridge. He couldn't see her expression, but from the hushed awe in her voice she seemed thrilled by the exact things he'd hoped would bore or dismay her.

"We'll walk from here," Tormod said, and helped her down before he dismounted.

"So the red deer keep to the ridges, and the pastureland is reserved for cattle, sheep and goats?" Jema asked as they followed the path to the village. "Does the laird demand a tithe from the villagers, or does he give them a percentage of the meat, wool and dairy products?"

If nothing else made it clear that Jema was from the future, her questions did. "Why does any of that matter to you?"

"I'm going to live here, so I should know

what to expect. Feudal system demands can be brutal on vassals, especially during famine or plague eras when…" She reappeared as she stopped in her tracks. "Tormod, if I'm from the future, how do I know all that?"

He wasn't going to admit that he didn't understand half of what she'd said, or how fetching he thought she looked dressed in skirts. "Mayhap you heard it in an old saga. Vikings must still sing in your time, surely."

"I don't know. I can't remember." She blew some air through her lips, startling the mare into making a similar sound, and then laughed. "But I can make funny noises, so maybe they do."

From the glen Tormod walked with her to the outskirts of the village, where he stopped to tether the mare to a road post. He pulled up the edge of the scarf to cover Jema's hair and most of her face.

"Dinnae speak to the villagers," he reminded her. "They must think you a maid come to walk with me."

Her smile slipped. "Do you go out with maids so often?"

"Not for walking so much," he admitted.

When she started to speak he held up his hand. "Be a maid, no' an inquisitor."

Jema scowled but nodded.

Tormod had seen her future world with its towering strongholds of glass and silver. From the strange lighted machines to the gleaming horseless carts that sped along the enormous web of roads, it was filled with endless marvels. He knew once she saw how hard the villagers worked and what little they had she would change her mind about returning to her time.

The first mortal they encountered was the village cooper, Tarven, who drove a cart filled with finished barrels.

"Fair morning to ye and yer lass, Marster," the cooper said, scowling as he touched his brow. "A grand day for a stroll, for them what can spare the hour."

"Are you for the stronghold, Tarven?" When the cooper nodded Tormod said, "Look in the kitchen when you've a moment. Cook wants new kegs for pickling, and I told her yours never leak."

Tarven's sour expression sweetened a little. "Thankee, Marster."

Once the cooper drove on Jema whispered, "What if he tells your cook about me?"

"He'll no' waste time gossiping when he can wheedle Cook to order new kegs," Tormod said. "Tarven loves coin above all, so now he's counting in his head what he'll make. By the time he arrives he'll have forgotten you." He nodded at the first cottage hemming the road into the village. "The people have to build their own houses here. Wattle and daub for the walls, and willow thatching for the roofs. You can hire help for it, but 'tis costly."

Jema glanced at the small, dingy house, and then at the two women working in the back of it. "Can you bid them fair morning?"

"Here men dinnae approach married women or their daughters without first asking permission of the man of the house." He pointed to the man scattering corn on the ground inside a pen filled with chickens. "Females have to be protected."

Jema regarded the husband. "Scottish women aren't taught to defend themselves?"

Tormod shrugged. "I cannae tell you that. But if you mean to stay here, lass, you'll be expected to wed and have bairns." He could do neither and would have to watch her with another man. He grit his teeth and ignored the bile rising in his throat. "Red tells me women of your time dinnae do so until they wish, and some never do."

Her expression grew thoughtful. "Why don't you have a wife or children?"

It was good that Jema hadn't pressed him about what she'd heard Diana say about him not seeming to age. Unless she was sworn to the clan, he was forbidden from telling her.

"I cannae have bairns, and I have naught to offer as a husband." He turned away from her. "Now come."

He took her first to the flax yard, where the weaver's wife and daughters turned the fibrous plant into strands.

"They let the flax ret there," he explained, pointing to the trench filled with stalks immersed in filthy, scum-covered stagnant water, the stench of which permeated the whole yard. "When they turn to tow, they are hung and dried until ready to separate. Beating them against iron hackling combs, over and over, forces the strands part. 'Tis bone-cracking work."

"But then they spin the strands into linen thread," Jema murmured. "This is something I could do. I've got strong arms, and organic linen is an amazing fabric."

The weaver's wife came out of the flax barn to bob before Tormod. "Are ye needing thread or wool, Marster? We've fine."

"Will you show my lass your hands, Mistress?" he asked.

The woman wiped them on her stained apron before holding them out. Thin white and pink scars latticed her palms and fingers, along with thick calluses on her fingertips from spinning. A fresh cut slashed across the pad of her thumb.

"I just gashed meself on the spindle," she explained, wriggling the wounded thumb. "We're all of us spinning for the loom now. Only tell Lady McDonnel she'll have her cloth by week's end, as promised."

"'Tis hard on the hands," Tormod said, and placed a coin in the woman's palm. "Our thanks, Mistress." He gave Jema a little push to start her walking.

"And ye want naught for it?" the weaver's

wife called after them. "Well, then, Marster, ye might gawp at me any day."

"I don't have as many scars, but my hands show that I work," Jema pointed out. "In fact, it's driving me mad to stay in your chamber every day all alone. Work will be good for me."

"Can you remember how to bake, and butcher? Did you work at a garden to grow food for your table, and herbs for medicine? Do you ken how to lay a fire?" When she said nothing he took her hand. "Jema, 'tis no' your willingness I question. 'Tis what you've no' done. You've no memory of your life, or how you worked, or what you ken. You have no people here to care for you."

Now she wouldn't look at him. "Show me the rest."

Tormod didn't spare her, but walked her to the butcher's slaughtering pen, the fish monger's gutting tables, and the baker's blazing hot outdoor ovens. Rather than show revulsion, each time she found something to admire. At last he went to his final stop, a tiny hut that had been cobbled together on the very edge of the road from the village.

Jema grimaced. "What's this place, and why is it all the way out here?"

"'Tis another future you should see. Only watch it from here, at the door." Tormod knocked, and waited for the old woman to call him before he entered. From his pack he took out a loaf of bread, a pot of jam and a bottle of cider, and placed it on the table beside the bed. "How do you fare today, Mistress McCallen?"

"As I ever do. Weeping and wretching up me lungs." Her toothless mouth stretched into a pained smile. "Never say ye brought me pottage again, ye rascal. The last pot 'twas so salty, it fair brined my gullet."

"I brought bread and jam, and the first press of cider from the tree by the fairy pool." Tormod touched her brow to check for fever, and then took her gnarled hand in his. Her fingernails had blackened, and open sores cratered the thin skin on her arms. But when he looked at her wrinkled face, he still saw the sweet, open-hearted lass she had been forty years past. "You dinnae have to be alone, Colblaith. Let Meg send a maid to care for you."

"So I might give a youngling the water elf sickness? I have me guards, and they're a-plenty." The old woman turned her head away and coughed into a rag, wheezing loudly before the spate abated. "The healer too comes every morn in his beaky mask to dose me and scold." Her gaze shifted. "Now there be a stunner."

He smiled a little as he used his dagger to slice the bread and spread some jam on it. He put the slice within her reach, and poured a cup of cider.

"You'll eat and drink for me now," he ordered.

"Aye, I'll do anything ye want, even still. I loved ye, lad." Colblaith grimaced. "I promised meself I'd never say such, no' after ye told me how it would be." She sighed and began to drift off. "How many like me have ye had? Dozens, hundreds?"

"One." As she closed her watery eyes, Tormod leaned over and kissed her brow. Beneath the sickbed odors she still smelled of the fields where she'd once tended the clan's sheep. "Rest now, Colblaith."

He covered her carefully with the blankets before he walked out and closed the door.

"That woman needs a doctor," Jema said flatly. "How can you just leave her in there like that?"

"This is where the villagers come to die," Tormod told her. "Colblaith came when the first spots appeared. She's well aware that she cannae survive it, and if others tend to her 'twill spread like fire. 'Tis a sickness that favors the young above all. Every bairn in the village would fall sick and die."

Jema looked over at two boys chasing after a dog with a stick clamped in its teeth.

"Even so, it's not right. No one should have to die alone."

"'Tis the way of it here. We've no medicines or doctors, no heart monitors or intensive care rooms. No clean white rooms or so many medicines we must stuff cabinets with them." He nodded grimly as she stared at him. "Aye, I saw such things in your time. The people of the future kept Red alive until we came for her. They've armies of healers to look after the sick and hurt. The hospital, it's a castle built for them and their care."

"But I'm not sick," she protested. "You're talking as if I'll keel over any moment."

"How do you ken you willnae? In your time you may live to be twice Colblaith's age. Here?" He pointed to the hut. "'Tis all you can hope if you are afflicted. That you die alone so you dinnae take others with you. I cannae save you from that, Jema. Naught can."

# Chapter Ten

NOW THAT GAVIN knew how to kill the undead, following the Romans deep into the forest didn't trouble him. He kept his dirk in one hand and the long spade in the other. He'd also taken the sword belonging to the soldier Fenella had killed and strapped it to his belt. He suspected he'd soon have to use both blades, judging by the sullen, hate-filled looks the men directed at her. She seemed oblivious to the danger she was in, something they would have to discuss once he dug up the treasure from the Viking's grave.

The Roman leading the others stopped at a wall of trees that had grown into each other. "This is the place, Prefect."

Gavin took a torch from one of the men and escorted Fenella up to the front of the formation, where she inspected the widest opening.

"The mortal and I will deal with the grave," she told the Romans. "Go raid that village we passed in the west valley. We shall need a dozen blood thralls for the journey back to Staffa."

Gavin's temper simmered as he watched the Romans march off. "They resent you, Mistress."

"I killed their leader. They want me dead." She looked up at him. "You neednae be afraid for me, lad. I'm too fast for them. Come now."

He followed her through the narrow entrance into a flower-covered space with a deep pit in the very center. It looked almost the same as the pit Jema had been working in just before they'd fallen through. And why did thinking of his sister make his head pound and his heart ache?

"There was no treasure buried here in my time," he said.

Fenella gave him an odd look, and walked over to the pit. She skirted around the edge until she saw something, and jumped down. "Here 'tis."

Gavin hoisted himself over the side, dropping down beside her. He buried the spade in the ground, and held up the torch to inspect the crumbling earth around them.

"There's nothing here," he said.

"'Tis what the Norse wish you to believe, a false grave."

Fenella swiped at the dirt wall in front of her, revealing thin, slotted stones. She pointed to the center, where the edges formed a starburst, and then slammed her fist against it. Broken chunks of thin stone pelted Gavin, who watched as the orthostats collapsed like a house of cards to reveal a second, deeper pit protected by an arched stone roof.

"How did you know it would do that?" he asked.

"A Norseman told me, before I ate him." She took his torch and ducked under the arch.

Gavin followed her into the crypt, which contained a long, low platform of logs surrounded by bundles of rotted cloth. Atop the platform lay a form covered by round shields that had rusted into each other.

"They didnae like this one," Fenella murmured as she lifted one of the shields. "See, thus? The body is chained to the logs. They feared this warrior would return from the grave."

Gavin only saw that Fenella was beautiful, even in this dismal place. He kicked at one of the bundles of decaying wool, from which a dusty object rolled. He bent to pick it up, and found it to be a curved choker of finely-worked gold set with polished ovals of amber, carved to resemble eyes.

Such a thing of beauty should have been placed on the Viking's body, not left on the bottom of the grave. The eyes looked so real he expected them to blink.

Fenella crouched and shoved the shields away from the chained skeleton. The anchors gave way from the spongy logs as soon as she tugged on them, but all that was revealed were gleaming ivory bones.

"Where is it?" She pushed the bones away to look beneath, and then hefted the skull to look inside it, and finally dropped it. "Facking bastart lied to me."

In a rage Fenella blurred around the room,

tearing apart the rest of the cloth bundles, which appeared to contain broken spear heads, seashells and a white sparkling powder.

Gavin wanted to comfort her and, as soon as she stopped, he brought her the jeweled neck piece. "Here."

Though he tried to give it to her, she waved it off. "Away with that. 'Tis no' the one."

But before she could turn from him, he gently slipped it around her long, pale neck. "A treasure befitting you, my lady."

Fenella shoved him away, ignoring the neck piece, and stared down at the skeletal remains of the Viking. "I cannae return to Staffa with empty hands. Quintus must have the map disc." She drove her boot into the pile of bones, crushing them.

Gavin saw a wisp of white dust rise from the shattered remains, and then another. "There is something inside them."

"Aye, death." She stomped on the skull, and then went still as a stream of dust fountained from the crushed eye sockets and swirled around her. Through it she stared at him, her eyes filled with horror. *"Gavin."*

He wanted to go to her, but his legs had gone numb, and the screeching sound inside his head was deafening him. Bile rose in his throat as he watched the dust cover her face, pouring into her ears and nose and mouth, until all of it had funneled inside her.

In the silence that followed the amber stones of the golden choker came alive and blinked at him, their gilded eyelids covered with sparkling amethyst crystals.

Dark brown streaks painted themselves in Fenella's bright hair, and when she opened her eyes they were no longer black, but a reddish-brown. She looked around her as if she were puzzled, and then focused on Gavin for a few moments. She glanced down at the shattered bones before she touched her face and gazed down at her body.

"This shall serve me well," she said and regarded him. Her voice had changed from Fenella's lilting soprano to a crystalline contralto. "Are you Pritani, guardsman?"

His paralysis vanished the moment she spoke, and his mind cleared. Gavin blinked and shook his head. "What did you do to Fenella?"

"Fenella?" she asked, but then nodded. "'Twas she who summoned me." Her slim hand stroked the golden neck piece. "That one 'tis gone though I have her memories. My torque called me back from Valhalla. Since she destroyed my body, I took hers." She flashed across the room to him. "I am Thora."

Here was his proof of an afterlife, yet Gavin found he didn't care. In fact, now that Fenella was gone, he couldn't remember why she had mattered.

"Thora," he repeated, as though he were waking from a dream. At their feet were the shattered bones that must have been hers. Around her long neck, her torque glittered in the torchlight. "Why did you come back?"

"To avenge my brother," she declared, the red flashing in her eyes. "He gave his life so that I might be free." For a moment her gaze took on a faraway look before her eyes snapped back to his face. "That debt will be repaid in Pritani blood." Though Gavin didn't know why the Pritani had slain this woman's brother, he pitied them. She cocked her head. "The Romans return. Too soon to have raided that village."

Flaming torches were hurled into the pit outside the hidden tomb.

"Show yourself, you murderous cunt," a voice called. "It is time you paid for your crimes against the legion."

"They, too, seek vengeance," Thora said. Without hesitation, she moved toward the tomb entrance.

Gavin put a restraining hand on her arm. "They mean to kill you."

Though her gaze rested on his hand for several moments, she finally looked him in the eye. "I ken it." When he let her go, she took the dirk from his hand, tested the blade, and nodded her approval.

Gavin didn't know much about Thora returned from Valhalla, but she was a soldier. Of that he was sure.

"Leave now," Thora called out to the Romans, "and keep your lives."

He moved to her side. "Even with your speed they have the advantage. They have the higher ground and control the only exit." A flaming log landed in the low arched entrance, followed by two more. "They mean to smoke us out."

"If you think that fire and smoke can stop me–"

Gavin shifted into camouflage mode. His body blended with the pit and also the flames that danced near its entrance. "I'll create a diversion," he said, and left her before she could object. He stepped around the logs and climbed out of the pit unnoticed.

"Pile more wood in there," one of the Romans sneered. "If she will not come out, it will become her tomb."

"I will go in and drag her out," a bigger man boasted. "She does not frighten me."

"You only wish to fuck her, Caro," another man chided.

The Roman chucking in the wood had lain his sword aside. Gavin snatched it up as he reappeared.

"Of course she frightens you," Gavin announced from behind them. The big man jumped straight up in the air but managed to turn as his three companions spun. "At least she'd frighten you if you had any brains."

"*You,*" said the man who was closest, brandishing his sword. He smiled a crooked, fanged smile. "Where is that bitch you serve?"

"Here," said Thora.

Gavin leapt forward and knocked aside his opponent's weapon with a downward slash. A quick upper thrust skewered the man's chest, which turned to ash, followed by the rest of him. Meanwhile the blur that was their former prefect swirled among the remaining Romans. They'd only barely begun to raise their weapons, when all three crumbled into gray heaps of ash.

Thora came to a stop beside him and looked down at the remains. "They were no' my enemies but they stood between me and my revenge." She used the toe of her boot to nudge the ashes. "For such there cannae be mercy."

There was no gleeful gloating in her voice, only more grim determination. Slowly it was dawning on Gavin that, despite her looks, this was not Fenella at all. She tucked the dirk behind her leather belt and studied him. Gavin had the distinct impression he'd not been found wanting.

"I see why the prefect favored you," she said and touched her torque. The amber eyes slowly closed. "I must journey north now, to the sea. You may accompany me, McShane, and serve as my personal guard."

He wiped the dust off his sword and pointed it at the horizon. "The sun will rise in twenty minutes. You're not going anywhere but the root cellar at the lodge until it sets. Unless you want to return to Valhalla as a burnt heap."

She grimaced but eyed the deeply purple horizon. Gavin watched as her reddish-brown eyes assessed the approaching dawn. She nodded tightly.

"I have waited this long, I can manage more."

"This way," he said and hustled her along the forest trail. They reached the lodge just as the first glimmer of sunlight came through the trees. He kicked the door open and ushered her in. As he slammed it shut he pointed to the cellar entrance. "Down there."

She disappeared in a whoosh down the stairs, while he grabbed the old blue tartan and a bundle of furs. Once he climbed down into the cellar, he wrapped the tartan around Thora and mounded the furs in a heap by the corner.

"This body is not alive," she told him. "It does not feel the cold as you do."

"Then give me the tartan," he suggested as he went over and sat down heavily on the furs. Though it was day outside, he found himself exhausted. Sleep would be welcome.

Thora came to stand over him. "Tonight we must travel. Once we reach the sea, we shall take a boat to a skerry off the coast. There I shall retrieve the instrument of my vengeance, and the debt I owe Tormod shall be paid."

Though Gavin had never said he would accompany her, the warrior from Valhalla was assuming it. Maybe she sensed the soldier in him, as he did in her. Or maybe it was simply the fact that she had no one else.

He nodded. "What's the name of this little island?"

"In my time, it had none." She sat down beside him, and with her finger drew the shape of an eye in the dirt floor. "But it looked like this."

## Chapter Eleven

THE LONG RIDE back to Dun Aran gave Jema plenty of time to think, but she was too upset to make any decisions. Once they left the village Tormod fell into a brooding silence that made her feel even more depressed. The Viking was her only ally in this world. She depended on his friendship. Why he was trying to scare her into returning to a time she couldn't remember didn't make sense. She knew he cared about her enough to rescue her, nurse her back to health, and hide her from the McDonnels. Why wouldn't he want her to stay? Life was ever a gamble, and he could get sick just as easily as…

"Tormod, if Mistress McCallen's sickness

is so contagious, why did you touch her and kiss her on the forehead?" Jema demanded.

"You saw much," he said, sounding a little amused. "I'll no' get the water elf sickness. I'm never ill."

"Is that right." Typical male arrogance, Jema thought, believing he was somehow indestructible. "If you happen to be wrong, who will take care of you?"

"Jema, hide," Tormod said suddenly.

As she cloaked herself in invisibility she saw the rider coming out of the ridges to intercept them. Tormod reined in the mare and waited for the other man, who wore the McDonnel tartan and had intricate, web-like tattoos on his neck and forearms.

"Did you see her?" the man asked without preamble.

"Aye. She's poorly. I left food and drink, but she'll likely want help with it." Tormod tossed a small sack to the other man, who rode on without a backward glance.

"That's what she meant by her 'guards,'" Jema said as Tormod guided the mare through the empty trail. But this close to the stronghold, she decided to stay invisible. "You've been sending other men from the clan to watch over her. I suppose they never get sick, either."

When he said nothing Jema's misery swelled and tightened into a gargantuan knot in her chest. Tormod didn't trust her. He didn't want her to stay. And all she was doing was making it worse.

Instead of dismounting outside the stronghold, the Viking rode the mare around the outer walls and into a large stable filled with horses. After looking around them, he dismounted.

"You can let me see you," he said reaching up for her. "Kalan is the stable master, but I've paid him to stay with Colblaith until dawn." He helped her down and nodded at the stair leading up to the hayloft. "Go up while I see to the nags. You can watch the sunset."

As she trudged up to the second level, Jema silently acknowledged that the Viking was right: she couldn't stay in his time. It was too savage and primitive, and she didn't have the spine to go it alone. Whatever pleasures or terrors the future might hold, at least there she might have some family and friends. Perhaps she'd discover she had a sweetheart who'd been going mad trying to find her.

Jema halted at the top step and blinked. The hayloft held plenty of hay, baled and stacked neatly against the walls, but someone had installed a huge bed directly across from a shuttered window. Was Kalan living up here?

Cloaking herself, she went to open the big shutter, which folded to one side to reveal a breathtaking view of the loch. From here she could see the width and breadth of the sapphire waters, and the high ridges on the opposite side of the deep crater. The pleasure of seeing more of the island's splendors made her body slowly rematerialize. No one would see her up here.

In one recessed cove steam danced in long curls above a white froth-capped pool. The thermal spring beneath the stronghold must have been supplying the heat. Beyond the vent a wide swath of blue flowers bloomed, which several shaggy young goats were busily cropping. Jema saw several tawny rabbits suddenly bound through the blooms, causing the skittish goats to bleat and hop away.

She turned her head and stopped breathing

as she saw the cause. Two large men carrying swords passed directly beneath her. She froze, but neither one looked up as they headed for the castle. It almost hurt to watch them go.

Even when she was visible, she was invisible.

Jema went over to the bed, which had been neatly made. The linens appeared new and clean, and smelled of sunshine and lavender. With a sigh she sat down on the edge, and then gingerly reclined. The mattress felt much thicker and denser than Tormod's bed. It cradled her back and hips like giant hands. Only then did she understand. This wasn't Kalan's bed. Tormod had made it for her. She would not be going back to his bedchamber.

A surge of exhaustion swamped Jema, who rolled over onto her side. Through watery eyes, she watched the sky turn all the shades of gold and pink as the sun sank toward the horizon. Soon she gave up the fight to remain awake and closed her eyes.

Sleep soothed away her despair, wrapping her in a quilt of soft darkness for a time. Gradually Jema felt the bite of damp chill, and huddled away from it, unwilling to wake to a world in which she was unwanted. Tomorrow she would tell her Viking she would return to her time, but for now she wanted one last, dreamless night in his.

Warmth crept over her shivering limbs, rousing Jema. She turned to it, pressing herself against a wall of hard muscle. It felt so delicious to soak up the heat pouring from the man holding her that she didn't bother to open her eyes or speak. She knew who he was, and she had spent too many nights wishing she could sleep in Tormod's arms. She wouldn't waste this arguing with him again. As surely as if he'd said it, she knew he was saying goodbye.

Her Viking held her loosely at first, one arm under her shoulder and the other curled around her waist. She could feel him cupping her nape, and stroking the center of it with his thumb. The fingertips of his other hand caressed the small of her back with such slow circles Jema doubted he realized he was doing it. As she nestled against him his arms tightened, as much to hold her to him as to eliminate the last of the spaces between their bodies.

She'd leave him tomorrow. Leave him to leap back into the abyss, when all she wanted was to be his.

"Jema." He made her name into another caress. "I am sorry I was short with you. I dinnae wish to let you go."

"Then don't. I could live away from the village," Jema whispered, and curled her fingers around the jut of his jawline to feel his heartbeat. "Up in the mountains, in a little hut, where no one will know about me but you. You can teach me how to raise goats and chickens and pigs."

His chest vibrated with a silent laugh. "Lass, I'm a map-maker, no' a farmer."

"I wish I knew what I was," she said and tucked her face against his neck and then turned her head. Strands of his long white-gold hair tangled with her eyelashes, but before she could free herself he tipped up her chin.

"You've blinded me," Jema murmured, closing her eyes.

"I ken the feeling." Gently he untangled

his hair from her, then pressed his lips to her brow. "You cannae go and live alone in a mountain hut. You shall freeze without me to build your fires."

"I like how you warm me now." Jema slid her hand up around his neck, bringing his face close to hers. When he stiffened she said, "Don't, please. Tomorrow I'll go. Tonight I need this. I need you."

A groan spilled from his mouth a moment before it took hers. He kissed her with utter ferocity, taking what she offered and demanding more, his lips and teeth and tongue marauding hers. He kissed her like a drowning man gulped air.

She wanted that. She wanted him to drown in her.

Jema didn't waste time with more talk, but turned over and urged him to roll with her, so that he lay atop her. When she cradled him with her thighs she felt the steely length of his erection press against her, throbbing with his heartbeat. She wanted his hands on her, and arched her back to rub her hard-peaked breasts against his chest. But the teasing press had the opposite effect.

Tormod rolled away from her and bolted off the bed.

"Wait," Jema said, sitting up. But she stopped when he tore off his tunic as if it were on fire. "Tormod?"

His hands knotted as he turned away from her and into the moonlight, which illuminated his shoulder. The lines of his tattoo glowed with icy light, and she felt the inside of her arm grow fiery hot. Then an unseen force dragged her arm up. She stared at it as an arrow of golden ink shot from her flesh, flashed through the air, and buried itself in the center of Tormod's tattoo.

"Oh my God," was all she could mutter, as a shooting star sliced through the sky behind him.

Heat flashed over her as if she had begun to burn from within, her body growing so hot she expected to see flames engulf her flesh.

"It's happening again," she gasped. "I swear to you, I'm not doing this–"

"I ken, lass," Tormod said as he staggered over to the bed. He reached for her with his shaking hands. "Dinnae fight it."

Afraid of what she might do, Jema avoided

his touch. His skin had gone white, making his eyes resemble blue ice and his hair sunlight on snow. She felt as if her insides were boiling, and saw the heat blooming over her in a dark rosy flush. She tore open the maid's gown, dragging it down to her waist as she gulped the chilly air.

The moonlight seemed to grow brighter as a resonant voice came out of her, and said in flawless Old Norse, "Before that which is now, the perfect silence of Ginnungagap, the nothing, was all. The chaos of what was and was not parted the realms of fire and ice. They came together with the nothing, and destroyed each other to create that which is. From fire and ice came the Aesir and the nine worlds. Came you, our valiant son."

Tormod's shoulders went rigid. "You marked Thora, no' me."

"The helm of hiding cannot be seen." She looked into his eyes, feeling terrified and assured all at once. "You gave it to this one as protection." Something lifted her hand to run the edge of her knuckles along his lean cheek. "Just as you gave your freedom for Thora, and your life for the children of the oaks."

"Please," he hissed. His fists bunched, and his body shook slightly, as if his self-control were about to snap. "Take me. Do as you will with me, no' my lady."

She leaned forward to kiss his brow. "We see you, son of Arn."

Jema's eyes widened as the golden arrow emerged from his big bicep, and darted between them, bouncing back and forth at first and then striking her like a shard of ice impaling her forearm. The arrow melted into her body, flattening back into an inked image.

Tormod dropped down beside her, his cold arms wrapping around her as the light from his tattoo faded. The moment her swollen breasts pressed against his stiff chest she felt the power inside her fade. She felt his body cool hers as she warmed his. Whatever had spoken through her was gone, but now she was weak and empty. She drew back to look at Tormod's shadow-masked face.

"What was that? You were trying to bargain with it, to save me from something."

"You were god-ridden. 'Tis when a Pritani spirit possesses the flesh of a mortal and speaks or acts in their stead. Only the spirit riding you was one of the Aesir, the Viking gods." He rubbed his hand over his face. "I offered myself to spare you."

"Spare me what?" She looked down at their fingers, which they had meshed together without even knowing. "What are they going to do to us?"

"It doesnae matter. I was never theirs." He lay back and pulled her down on him, shifting her until her limbs draped over his. "And they cannae have you."

Jema felt suddenly, ridiculously pleased. "You *did* call me your lady."

"Are you no'?" He gripped the back of her head and guided her lips to within a breath of his. "I'm yours, if you'll have me."

Jema felt the heat return inside her body, but this time it was soft and deep and wet. She watched his face as she reached down to tug at the fabric bunched around her waist. It took some twisting and wriggling before she could toss the gown away and stretch out naked atop him.

"Where were we? Oh, I remember." She bent her head to his, and whispered a kiss over his lips. "I'm having you."

Kissing Tormod occupied Jema for a time, perhaps because she'd thought about it so often. She loved how their lips fit together, and the taste of him, cool and almost sweet. When she teased his tongue with hers he groaned, and his hands slid down the length of her back to cup her bottom. She rubbed her breasts gently against his chest, enjoying the way he jerked when her engorged nipples grazed his.

She took her mouth from his as she felt his muscles bunching under her, and sensed he was about to go for what he wanted. "You're too impatient."

"You're naked, and I'm a man." He rolled over with her, pinning her under him and framing her face with his hands. "And look at you. You're as tempting as a chest of jewels, you smell of firelight and you taste of…" He kissed her. "Wild cherries and cream, only more luscious."

"Now you're making *me* impatient." She reached behind him to untie his trouser laces, and stopped as she realized something. "I don't know if I've ever been with a man. It's not as if I can go and get a physical." She met his gaze. "Would it matter?"

His expression softened. "You're with me now, lass. Naught else matters."

Jema tugged down his trousers, and spread her thighs so that his thick, heavy erection pressed against her slick folds.

Tormod drew her knees up around his narrow hips, and reached between them to fist his shaft and guide his swollen glans to her. Once he notched himself just inside her opening, he stroked her trembling thigh.

"You've naught to fear, lass. Give over to me. Aye, that's my Jema." He pressed in until the satiny bulb of his cockhead had penetrated her. "Let me inside, *kona.* I'll love your pretty quim as you need me, aye."

He kept murmuring to her as he worked his length into her, inch by aching inch. He felt much bigger and thicker and harder than she'd expected. If she hadn't been so wet with arousal the merging would have been painful, their fit was so tight. At last he buried himself deep inside her.

Jema felt deliciously stretched and impaled, and then she saw how tight his jaw was, and the set of his shoulders. "Tormod?"

"Dinnae move," he whispered harshly.

Slowly he slid back out of her, and then penetrated her again. "Do I hurt you?" When she shook her head he exhaled heavily. "Hold onto me, lass. I cannae wait another breath."

Jema gasped as he began to stroke in and out of her, his hips pounding with such force her breasts bounced. At the same time he worked his hands under her buttocks, squeezing them as he pumped into her pussy. His head bowed, and his mouth fastened over one peak, sucking and licking in time with the hammering rhythm of his hips. He tormented one mound and then the other, until Jema thought her tight nipples would burst.

He fucked her steadily and mercilessly, and her body responded with the same mindless passion, thrusting with him and gripping him from inside. She jutted her breasts against his hungry mouth, and knotted her hands in his hair, crying out as the need inside her grew impossibly huge.

Tormod plowed deep into the core of her, and that one brutal thrust pushed her over the edge. Jema fell back into the darkness, only now it was hot and heavy and filled with him. The pleasure made her drag down his head for a kiss to stop her from crying out with the joy of it.

Tormod pushed into her again, his big body jerking, and Jema couldn't stop coming, not with him flooding her with his thick, warm seed. They held each other inside that storm of bliss, until it rolled away and they collapsed, unable to do more than gasp and shake.

Her Viking recovered enough to disengage their bodies and shift over to her side. He placed his hand on her damp belly, and looked down at her with the same astonished appreciation she felt.

"I dinnae think you are a maiden," he said, very gravely.

Laughter bubbled out of her, and she curled up against him, holding him close as he shared her mirth. Then his hands found her bottom again, which made her curl a leg over his hip and slide her soaked sex against his slick shaft.

"You may want to check me again," Jema told him, "Just in case you missed something the first time."

"Gods, you are a generous lass." He cupped her bottom and massaged the tight curves before he rubbed his thumb over the pucker of her rosebud. "You may regret offering."

While her virginity was a non-issue, Jema felt sure she had never been with a man like him. He made love the way a warrior went into battle. His body was a weapon of pleasure, his focus complete. What he wanted he could have, too. The moment he'd slid into her she'd finally let go of all her fears. She wanted to have him again and again, because as long as he was inside her she felt as if she could conquer the world.

"Anything you want," she said against his jaw. "I'm yours, Viking."

Tormod dragged her over onto her belly, jerking up her hips and burying his mouth against her pulsing sex. As he penetrated her with his tongue, Jema pressed her face against the pillow to stifle the moans spilling from her lips. The sensations flashed through her, as bright and hot as a shower of white-hot sparks.

"Please," she begged, not sure what she needed, but confident he could give it to her.

Tormod found her clit with the edge of his

teeth, grazing the swollen pearl before he sucked and licked, laving it while he worked his thumb against her bottom pucker, pressing it just enough to make her gasp.

"Wild cherries," he muttered as he hauled her back against him, cupping her breasts. With one hard thrust he was inside her, and worked her mounds in time with the pounding he gave her spasming pussy. Next to her ear he crooned, "I'm your cream now, wench."

Jema gripped the sides of his thighs, digging her nails into his flexing muscles as she tightened around him, massaging him from within each time he plowed into her. She felt his chest heave, and heard him make a hoarse sound. She impaled herself on him, leaning back until her head rested against his shoulder.

"So you're mine, are you?" he said, his voice low and soft, "I'll no' leave you alone again, my lass. You'll come to crave this every night, as I have, watching you sleep. And you'll take me now, willnae you?"

His sensual threat almost shattered her again. "Yes. Oh, Tormod."

The climax that seized and shook her

wouldn't let go, and he swore as he drove hard and heavy into her, gripping her breasts as his cock swelled and pumped. Finally she fell limp and boneless, and he tumbled with her, their arms and legs tangled. The aftershocks racked them as if they were fevered, and then at last the cold night air soothed their flushed, sweat-sheened bodies.

Jema could feel his big body relax as he dozed, his shaft still firmly planted inside her, and pillowed her cheek on his hand. She'd be tender in the morning, but she didn't care. If she could hold him inside her until they woke, they could start the day as they'd ended it.

Tormod was wrong. She already craved him. She also realized why she couldn't go back to her time, and it had nothing to do with the loss of her memory.

She'd fallen utterly, hopelessly, and irreversibly in love with her Viking.

## Chapter Twelve

RACHEL TALORC BRAIDED her long dark hair as she watched her husband finish dressing for his night duty. "Are you sure I can't tag along? Maybe I can pick up something from the Viking."

Evander belted his tartan before he buckled the spear sheath strap across his chest. "We agreed you're no' to read the minds of the clan. Liefson maynae be Pritani, but he fought like one with us against the Romans. For that he deserves the same consideration."

"He also didn't kill you on the black ship when you were trying to free me from the legion," she reminded him. "And he supported you rejoining the clan and becoming Captain of the Guard. I want to help him. I'll just take a quick look."

His slanted green eyes glittered as he came to take her in his strong arms. "I dinnae have to read minds to ken that you've been conniving with Raen's wife."

Rachel tilted her head back to smile at his fierce, handsome face. "She didn't kill you either."

Evander lifted her off her feet, and kissed her until she clutched his shoulders and tried to wrap her legs around his waist. "More of that and I'll no' leave this chamber until dawn." He held her for a moment longer before he set her down. "'Twill only be a few hours before I return. Be naked for me when I do."

A few minutes after Evander left, a knock sounded. Rachel went to let Diana inside. "He said not to read the Viking, and he meant it."

"Despite once being a real jerk, your husband is a very good guy." The towering redhead closed the door and leaned back against it. "Here's the thing: I'm not that good, and neither are you. Something's wrong, very wrong, and if we don't get on top of it–"

"Tormod will leave the clan. I know, you told me." Rachel touched her arm. "Maybe that's not such a terrible thing. He isn't like the rest of the McDonnels. If he goes back to Norway, he'll find what he's been missing."

"You really think there's a clan of immortal raiders hanging out in the fjords? And they will welcome their brother, the Scottish Viking, with open arms?" Diana threw up her hands. "This is something else, Rache. I swear to you, all my cop gauges are in the red. You have to read him and find out what it is."

She felt all the emotions flooding out of her friend, and some of them made sense of her urgency. "Does Tharaen know how close you came to falling in love with Tormod?"

"Oh, sure. I told him that on our wedding night." Diana made a rude sound. "Don't get any ideas. It's Raen for me, it always has been. Forever won't be long enough for us. But the Viking is mine, too. My best friend, and my honorary big brother, and the family I never got in my time. Of course I love the jackass. Now will you peek inside his brain and tell me what the fuck is wrong with him?"

Rachel knew her friend didn't realize she

was shouting. Nor could she explain to Diana how her spirit-bond with Evander through his ink made it almost impossible for her to go against his wishes. "I can't disobey my husband. I'm sorry."

Without another word Diana stalked out of the chamber, slamming the door behind her.

Worried that her friend might do something even more reckless, Rachel pulled on her cloak and went to find her husband, whom she tracked by his cool, decisive thoughts, to which she was permanently connected. He had stopped in the armory to have a word with Neacal Uthar about forging some special spear heads. For a time she nervously paced along the gallery, until she saw Evander enter below. Though he bounded up the steps in front of her, she thought she heard something like footsteps approaching from behind. But before she could look, Evander was with her.

"I thought you were keeping the bed warm, wife," he teased, and then stopped suddenly. Taking the spear from his shoulder sheath, Evander quickly put her behind him, ready to throw. When she rested her hand on his arm, he told her quietly, "No." In a louder, commanding tone he said, "Show yourself."

Although the gallery remained empty except for the two of them, Rachel felt a third person's presence. Which was impossible, unless the intruder was a ghost.

*Or invisible.*

A flood of fear was pouring over her from her husband's immediate right.

"I can't see anyone here, my love," she said, turning in that direction.

"Nor I." Slowly he lowered the spear, and gave her a rueful look. "I thought I smelled the Viking, and a female. But 'tis no' like him to chase after a maid through the stronghold." He came and put his arm around her. "What do you here, now that I have terrified you?"

"Diana was upset with me for refusing to read Tormod." Telling one truth but not another was better than lying twice. "I told her you asked me not to, so I thought I should warn you that she is now upset with *you*."

"That explains why she didnae return my greeting when we passed in the kitchens. I'll speak with her." He caressed her cheek. "Go to bed, love. I'll wake you later."

Rachel nodded, and started walking in the direction of their bed chamber. As soon as Evander turned the corner, she backtracked and opened her mind. The thoughts of the hidden female were lightened by relief and muddled by regret.

*Tormod is going to be so angry.*

"You didn't do anything wrong," she told the unseen woman. "My husband has a very keen sense of smell. What's your name?"

The woman's fear spiked.

"It's okay, you don't have to tell me." Rachel lifted her hands in a gesture of surrender. "Mine's Rachel. Are you lost?"

*I know where I am, but I can't remember my name. Tormod calls me Jema.*

The unseen woman was deliberately thinking her answers, which gave Rachel a small amount of hope.

"Jema, I'm going to a room where we can speak without drawing any attention. You don't have to show yourself, and I'll leave the door open, too."

Walking away from Jema gave Rachel a few moments to think. Something definitely seemed amiss with the other woman. Jema's thoughts felt clear and strong, but behind them was a layer of dark emotion between her consciousness and a lifetime of memories.

Rachel entered the map room, and went to stand by the window. If Jema was Tormod's secret, then it would explain a great deal. The Viking had a very protective nature, as well as a tendency to mischief.

The door to the chamber slowly closed.

"You're the mind reader," a low voice said in a distinct Scottish accent. "That's how you knew I was there."

"Yes, and I heard your footsteps." Rachel gestured toward the work table. "Would you like to sit down?"

One of the chairs slid out, and rocked a little.

Carefully Rachel approached from the other side and sat down. "Jema, how long have you been at Dun Aran?"

"I don't know. I haven't a calendar." Her voice went low as she added, "I think it's been two weeks, maybe a bit longer."

Rachel nodded. "It's a little disconcerting, talking to thin air. Can you make yourself visible?"

The emptiness of the chair gradually became filled with the transparent form of a fair-haired, lovely young woman with worried eyes and a tight mouth. She appeared more Scandinavian than Scots, especially with her striking bone structure and coloring. Her I'D RATHER BE DIGGING t-shirt made Rachel smile, until she realized what it meant.

"You're from the future," Rachel blurted out. She hadn't meant to be that blunt, but it seemed to put Jema at ease. "Sorry, it's just a little exciting. There are only three of us here. Now four, with you."

The other woman leaned forward. "Did you know me in our time? Have you ever seen me?"

"No," Rachel said and felt a bitter surge of disappointment from the other woman. "But I think I can help you." She recalled how she had looked into Cailean's mind in order to save Evander. "I don't think your memories are gone. I think they're blocked." She eyed the fresh scar on Jema's temple. "Did you hit your head after you came here?"

"It happened before I came, or on the way." She touched the spot. "I woke up bleeding in Tormod's arms. What did this, I can't tell you. How can you help?"

"There are levels to my ability," Rachel told her. "I've been reading only your active thoughts. I can use a deeper reach and try to read your blocked memories. It may free them so you can remember your past."

Jema slowly nodded. "But you've never done this."

"Not with someone who has amnesia," Rachel admitted. "If you feel any pain, or want me to stop at any time, I will." She held out her hands over the table. "It works best if I can touch you."

The other woman didn't hesitate, and joined hands with hers. "All right."

Rachel closed her eyes in order to concentrate entirely on Jema's mind. Her active thoughts had gone still, and were laced with fear, but she didn't resist Rachel's reach. The dark wall of emotions did, pushing at her as she encountered it, but she persisted with gentle determination.

Around the edges of the wall images began to slip by, all of Jema working outdoors. She did like to dig. In fact, she dug big holes in the ground, huge trenches, carefully excavated. She came out of them to search through screens of soil, and study bits of pottery and chipped stone she'd bagged and numbered. With the field work images came a stream of texts, illustrations and lectures from Jema's years as a student. Hundreds of nights spent in the library, always studying alone, and the bright pleasure of the day she'd received her first degree.

"You're an archaeologist," Rachel murmured, smiling a little as she watched a memory of Jema sharing tea with other helpers at a site in the lowlands. "That's why you'd rather be digging."

As more memories circumvented the wall, the darkness began to thin. Rachel relived the morning when Jema had learned her parents had been killed, and the bleak double funeral that followed. At her side had been a massive soldier in a black-cuffed red coat, high feathered helmet and dark green kilt, who had held her hand through the service.

"Gavin," Jema whispered.

The dark wall collapsed, and Rachel saw Jema's twin brother as a boy, chasing her through a field of heather. They had grown up as each other's best friend, separated only when Gavin had chosen to join the military. Her heart clenched as she experienced Jema's devastation when Gavin had finally revealed the reason for his medical discharge from The Black Watch: ALS. From that day on Jema had devoted herself to caring for her twin as his condition deteriorated.

Rachel walked with Jema and Gavin as they visited her last dig, and watched as events unfolded. Jema's head injury had not blocked off her memories. It had been the horror she'd felt to see Gavin falling in the pit after her. Rachel gasped as she watched the twins hurtle back in time. Then everything went dark until Jema opened her eyes and saw Tormod for the first time.

The release of her hands cut off Rachel's reach, and she opened her eyes to see Jema standing and holding her head as tears streamed down her face. On impulse she came around the table to embrace the other woman, and held her until she calmed.

"I killed him," Jema finally managed to get out. She stepped back, frantically shaking her head. "Gavin's dead, and it's all my fault."

"I don't think so," Rachel said and touched her shoulder. "You both came back to this time through a sacred oak grove that has the power to heal."

The other woman's silvered blue eyes widened for a moment, and then she shook her head. "I wasn't healed. I came out of the pit hurt and bleeding."

"Maybe Gavin was the one to be healed," Rachel told her. "You remember him crossing over with you, but you never found his body."

"I didn't look for him," Jema said, sounding ashamed now. "I didn't remember him at all."

"Your head injury, combined with seeing Gavin fall, is likely what blocked off your memories. You couldn't remember him because you thought he was dead. It would have broken your heart." Rachel wished she knew more about the function of the sacred groves. "I need to talk to the druids about what happened to you. I'd also like to introduce you to the other women from our time. We can help you find your brother, I promise."

Jema gave her a stricken look. "Do you really think it's possible that Gavin's still alive? That he's been healed?"

"Oh, yes," Rachel said, and smiled. "I know it's possible because I was."

❧

While Rachel went to fetch Kinley and Diana, Jema cloaked herself and sat staring at the map wall. Having her memories restored felt almost as wonderful as the prospect that Gavin might still be alive. It also made her feel sick to imagine him wandering the forest lost and alone, unaware that they'd time-traveled to the fourteenth century.

And then there was Tormod, who knew none of this, or her.

She didn't regret a moment she'd spent with her Viking, but what would he think of her exposing herself to Rachel and the other women?

A wave of panic made her hurry to the door, only to stumble backward as Diana Aber strode in, followed by a slender blonde in an emerald silk gown. As Rachel came in Jema hurried to press herself against the nearest wall and listen.

"If you and Kinley plan to give me more grief about Tormod," the redhead said to Rachel, "I'm out of here."

"This is something else." Rachel closed the door and looked around the room before she gestured for the other women to sit. When neither one did, she said, "There's another woman who has crossed over from the future. She's here, now, at Dun Aran."

"What?" Kinley said immediately. "Who is she? When did she arrive?"

"And where have you been hiding her?" Diana drawled. "Because a cricket can't get inside this place since your husband beefed up the patrols and guards."

Rachel glanced around the room. "Jema, maybe you should answer that."

She walked over to stand between the women before she uncloaked. "She didn't have to hide me. I'm very hard to find."

Kinley blinked, and Diana uttered a sharp sound. Both women stared at Rachel in disbelief.

"Allow me to introduce Dr. Jema

McShane, an archaeologist with the National Trust in our time," Rachel said, and smiled at her. "Jema, this is Lady Kinley McDonnel, the laird's wife, and formerly an Air Force Captain who worked search and rescue in combat zones. Diana Aber, our clan tracker, was a detective with the San Diego police department, assigned to missing persons."

Jema nodded. "Pleasure."

Kinley offered her hand, and when she clasped it said, "I crossed over while on a therapeutic outing with my shrink from a VA hospital. Diana fell through while she was trying to track me down, and poor Rachel was buried alive. How did you end up here?"

"A trench at the dig in the highlands I was working collapsed." She grimaced. "I hit my head and lost my memory. Tormod found me when I came through, and brought me here to look after me."

"We think Jema's brother Gavin also crossed over," Rachel put in, and explained what she'd seen in Jema's memories. "Diana, do you think you might be able to track him down?"

"How long has it been since you got

here?" the redhead asked, and when Jema gave her an estimate she sighed. "Yeah, I should be able to pick up his trail." She nodded at Jema's feet. "Just FYI: don't get lost, Scotty, because you don't leave a trail at all."

Jema's lips twitched at the new nickname. "I'll try to remember that, Red."

"So this is what that sun-bleached bastard has been hiding for the last two weeks," Diana said and regarded Kinley. "You need to speak to Lachlan about finding the brother."

"Wait, I only just met you three," Jema protested. "I need to talk to Tormod about this, too."

"So do I, sweetheart," the redhead said as she headed for the door. "I'll see you ladies after I beat the snot out of a Viking."

"Let her go," Kinley told Rachel when she made as if to go after her. To Jema she said, "She needs to yell at Tormod. It'll be good for both of them. As for you, we have to go see my husband now." She held up her hand when Jema started to protest. "I know you're scared. When I first got here I was, too. Diana shot a druid her first night at Dun Aran."

"Which was an accident," Rachel said quickly.

"The point is, if we're going to find your brother, we need the clan." The laird's wife met Jema's gaze. "And the clan belongs to Lachlan."

Jema nodded, and reluctantly accompanied the two women to the laird's tower. With every step she took she wanted to cloak herself, and run to tell Tormod everything she remembered. She also worried what Diana might do to her Viking. If she hurt Tormod then she'd have to square off with the cop, and Jema had no doubt that Diana would be the winner.

Rachel burst into a laugh, and then gave her an apologetic look. "Diana isn't violent at all. She'll scold Tormod until his ears burn, but he really is her best friend."

"I know what you mean. Gavin is mine." Jema felt her stomach knot as two clansmen passed them and stared at her. "Am I in trouble for staying at the castle without permission?"

"Not at all," Kinley said as she climbed the last flight of stairs and stopped in front of a huge chamber. "You didn't choose to come here. The Viking brought you. We don't punish druid kind for being injured or having amnesia, either."

Inside the chamber was a big room with rounded walls that contained an enormous bed and a number of primitive but well-made furnishings. Behind a table covered with scrolls stood two of the biggest men Jema had ever seen.

"Gentlemen," Rachel said, smiling as if everything were completely normal. "Allow me to introduce Jema McShane, from twenty-first century Scotland. Jema, meet Lachlan McDonnel, laird of the clan, and Tharaen Aber, Dun Aran's seneschal."

"My lords." Jema bobbed in what she hoped was a respectful curtsey.

Raen came around the table to loom over her. "Are you armed?"

"No, sir." Jema felt bewildered.

He smiled a little. "Since my wife came with weapons I must ask." He regarded her t-shirt. "What do you dig?"

"Ditches," Kinley answered for her. To her husband she said, "Lachlan, Jema came through a forest portal in the highlands. Her brother came with her, and may still be there looking for her."

"We'll send a warband tomorrow to search for him." The laird turned to Jema. "Did you journey here by yourself, my lady?"

"No, my lord." She cleared her throat. "Tormod Liefson found me after I crossed over. He brought me here."

"Did he." Lachlan's dark eyes narrowed, and he exchanged a flinty look with Raen before he asked, "When was this, my lady?"

"I'm not sure," she said and smiled. "You're obviously busy, so I'll go. I appreciate anything you can do to help locate my–"

"She's been here for two weeks, maybe longer," Kinley told her husband. "Tormod had her hidden somewhere. Probably in his chambers."

"I'm sure he only wanted to protect Jema," Rachel said quickly. "She was injured, and lost her memory."

"Find the Viking," the laird told Raen, in the same tone he might have said *Kill him*. To Jema he said, "Come downstairs, my lady, and we shall discuss with my chieftains how best to find your brother."

Jema felt only too aware of the guards that followed them from the laird's tower chamber. She also sensed Raen watching her, and glanced to see the suspicion in his eyes, as if he expected her to jump Lachlan any moment. While Kinley spoke in low tones with her husband, Rachel stayed by Jema's side and talked about Dun Aran as if they were on a tour of the place.

"The great hall is where the clan has their meals and socializes." She gestured toward some tables with checkerboard tops. "The men like to play a form of checkers called quoits, but I'm teaching a few of them chess."

"What happens to me and Gavin, once we find him?" she couldn't help asking Rachel.

"We'll help you get back to your time, or find a place for you here." Rachel's expression turned shrewd. "Were you and Tormod planning to go off together?"

"You know we were," Jema replied. There didn't seem to be much point in lying to a mind-reader.

They reached the center of the great hall,

where Lachlan called to the clansmen who were present to gather around them.

"Can we send for Tormod?" Jema asked Rachel. "He knows the place where Gavin and I crossed over in the forest."

"You mean, you want to warn him to go before he has to face the consequences," Rachel said as she looked past her and lit up with glowing happiness. "Here's Evander. I'd like to introduce you, if you wouldn't mind."

"Of course," Jema said.

But when she turned to look at Rachel's tall, copper-haired husband she shriveled a bit inside. The Captain of the Guard looked every bit as big and fierce as the other McDonnels, but possessed an air of focused intensity that made her take a step back.

"Our intruder from the future," Evander said once his wife had performed the introductions. "Have you been ill-used while you've been at Dun Aran, my lady?"

"No, Captain." Belatedly she realized he must smell Tormod's herbal salt soap on her hair and skin. "I've been very well looked after since I came here."

He didn't say anything as he watched her

face. At last he nodded, kissed his wife, and made his way through the gathered men to talk to the laird.

"Evander can be a little intimidating," Rachel said. "But under all that dark, lethal warrior persona he's a good and kind soul."

Jema was pretty sure he was the most dangerous man she'd ever met. "I'll take your word for it."

Rachel introduced her to other members of the clan, many of whom shared the last name Uthar. She and Rachel talked with several warband leaders about the highland forest, and how the ancient Vikings had protected their warrior's burial site. The voices around them went still as the laird called out, "Bring him to me."

Jema forgot to breathe as she saw Raen and one of the Uthars march Tormod up to Lachlan. She gripped Rachel's arm. "What are they doing?"

"Tormod must answer for concealing you from the clan," the other woman said.

"I'm told you left the island without permission to go seeking a grave," the laird said, his tone harsh. "There you found this woman, and brought her back to Dun Aran, also without leave. You told no one of her, but hid her from us. 'Tis true?"

"Aye, my lord." The Viking's expression remained impassive. "As I told your seneschal, I plan to return to Norrvegr. When I do, I'll take the wench with me."

"You took an oath of loyalty to the laird," Raen said, growling the words. "You swore to protect the clan above all, or have you forgotten?"

Tormod shrugged.

Evander leaned close to him, looking all over his face. "The wench is a lady, and she smells of you. Did you force yourself on her? Is that why you've kept her locked away in your chamber?"

"I dinnae hurt females, Talorc," Tormod said, sounding just as threatening. "A pity you couldnae say the same before you took Rachel from a portal, and hid her away in the highlands."

Neither man backed off, and for a moment Jema thought they might come to blows. Then the captain looked at his wife, and stepped to one side.

"We have to stop this, now," Jema told Rachel.

The other woman shook her head. "This is clan business. We can't interfere." In a lower voice she said, "But later *I* might beat the snot out of your Viking."

"Wait. Wait just a damn minute." Diana appeared, and waded her way through the men to reach Lachlan. "Tormod found an injured woman, my lord, and brought her here to nurse her back to health. She's druid kind, or she wouldn't have come through the portal." She looked at the grim faces around her. "I know he's a pain in the ass, but that has to count for something."

"No' when he betrayed his oath to do it," the laird finally said. "Evander, take him to the dungeon."

## Chapter Thirteen

CAILEAN LUSK ENTERED the McDonnel's stronghold with his master, Bhaltair Flen, to find dozens of clansmen assembled in the great hall. Nearly all of them were trying to talk at the same time, their voices edged with anger and indignation. In the center of the uproar stood Lachlan McDonnel, his most trusted men, and their wives, all of whom were trying to calm the uproar. Around the edges the McDonnel's chatelaine and her maids hovered, all snarling their aprons with their hands.

"I see the cause of this." Bhaltair pointed at a fourth, unfamiliar female dressed in garments from a future era. "Our watchers on the island should have reported her crossing to us."

"I had word from them yesterday, Master," Cailean said, frowning at the strange female. "No one has come through the portal on Skye since Lady Kinley brought back Lady Diana."

"Dinnae remind me of what a fool I have been, I beg you." The older druid peered again. "This one has the look of a Norsewoman. Do you see the quality of the eyes?"

Cailean winced. Druids did not breed with the Viking peoples for many reasons, the primary being that their magics had proven highly incompatible. "She could be Francian. They are known to be quite fair in the northern lands."

His master grunted. "The gods bedevil us once more. Come, lad."

Agitated as they were, the clan still made way for them, and fell silent in their wake. Cailean kept his expression impassive as his master greeted the laird, but he could not stop watching the fair woman. She possessed the gentle green aura of druid kind, but something else flickered through it. He saw it as flame one moment, and a golden arrow the next.

"We regret our intrusion," Bhaltair was saying to the laird, "but reports of a troubling nature have come to us. The conclave bid us come to advise you."

Lachlan held up his hand, and glanced around at his men. "All that has been said for and against Tormod Liefson will be considered. In the morning I shall advise your chieftains on what is to be done. Return to your duties now, and speak no more of this."

The McDonnels collectively grumbled, but no one spoke against the laird. Slowly the men trudged out of the hall.

Kinley summoned Meg Talley, the castle's chatelaine, and asked her to bring hot brews for the druids. To Cailean she said, "Should we talk here, or in the tower?"

Although she should have asked his master for his preference, Cailean knew the bloodline they shared made her inclined to defer to him. "'Tis a matter we may discuss here, I think." He glanced at Bhaltair, who nodded his approval. "May we greet your guest?"

"Sure," Kinley said and turned to the fair

woman. "Jema, these are our druid friends, Ovate Cailean Lusk and Master Bhaltair Flen. Gentlemen, this is Jema McShane, who oddly enough is not American or from San Diego."

The fair woman eyed him with a healthy amount of wariness. "You're an actual druid?"

Her Scottish accent gave him pause, but only for a moment. "Aye, Mistress. Please know that you are very welcome among us."

Diana folded her arms. "Oh, *now* you're a welcoming committee. How come I didn't get one when I fell through the looking glass?"

"You shot me with your gun," Bhaltair said, smiling fondly at the redhead. "I was too occupied with bleeding."

Once Meg brought hot mugs of herb brew for the druids, the McDonnels gathered around the largest table to listen to the druids' latest reports of undead activity.

"Quintus Seneca's female guard, known to us as Fenella Ivar, has been seen traveling in the highlands," Bhaltair told the laird. "She is accompanied by an enslaved male who has the ability to vanish from sight by blending in with his surroundings. The male is Scottish, but speaks strangely. He also wears clothing that from the descriptions clearly comes from the future."

Jema went rigid. "Gavin is a *slave*?"

"The man may be Gavin McShane, Jema's twin brother," Rachel explained to the old man. "She believes they crossed over together through a highland forest portal, and then were separated."

"However he came here, the man is quite powerful, and very protective of his mistress." Bhaltair related some of the pair's attacks on different villages as they travelled through the highlands. "At present they are moving north. Last night they stole a pair of horses from an estate not twenty miles from the coast. Fenella is also actively enthralling more mortals and sending them west. For what purpose, we cannae tell you, but we have a list of where they have been seen."

The laird suggested they adjourn to the map room, but as the others followed Lachlan and Bhaltair, Cailean lagged behind to accompany Jema.

"You must have many questions about our people," he said to her. "I am happy to explain what I may."

"I don't care about being a druid," she snapped, but then she stopped and took in a deep breath. "I'm sorry, that was rude. It would be better if you can tell me how and why my brother was enslaved by an undead Roman woman."

"In years past 'twas common for the legion to abduct and imprison mortals, so they had a steady supply of blood," Cailean said. "In these last years they have discovered the means with which to enslave their will absolutely. Now those they take are happy to serve as minions and guards." Since they were speaking about her brother's fate, he decided not to tell her about how thralls were also used for sex. "We have learned that the unnatural influence can be broken if the undead who enthralled the mortal is killed."

Jema's mouth tightened. "Good. Then all I have to do is stab her in the chest."

"In the heart," he gently corrected. "Or you may cut the throat deeply, sever the spine, crush the brain, or set the undead to burn." He saw her horror and cleared his throat. "May you never have to encounter the legion,

Mistress McShane, but should you, 'tis better you ken how to end them."

In the map room Bhaltair read off the locations of the sightings, which Diana marked on the wall with chalked circles.

"Looks like the mortals are headed straight to Morven," Diana said. The redhead stepped back from the wall to study the marks to the east. "Fenella and Jema's brother are moving due north, to the sea." She marked a spot on the coast. "If they don't change direction, they'll end up here."

"We've had no reports of undead attacks or missing mortals in that region," Raen pointed out.

"Aye, and Seneca hasnae the men nor the resources to build a new stronghold beneath our notice. He would need a great many thralls." Lachlan regarded the redhead. "What do you think, Diana?"

"We sank two of their black ships, but they probably had more." She tapped some of the islands off the coast. "The Orkneys would be my pick for an undead hide out. Lots of sea caves, water all around, and the mortals are cut off from the mainland."

Kinley nodded. "With the smaller populations, they could easily enslave an entire island, and no one would be the wiser." She looked at Cailean. "Are there any druid tribes living on the islands that we can message by bird?"

"None, my lady." The ovate's stomach churned as ugly memories flashed through his thoughts. "The Moon Wake tribe once dwelled on Everbay, but they were massacred by raiders some twenty years past."

"What will happen to my brother?" Jema suddenly demanded.

Bhaltair nodded to Cailean, who said, "Most thralls now are kept alive to serve their undead masters. A few are killed protecting them from warbands, or die because they have been bled too often."

Jema shook her head, backing away from the wall map, as her face blanched. Diana hurried to her side, grabbed an empty scroll case, and opened it in time for the other woman to wretch into it.

"We're talking about her twin brother, guys," the redhead snapped. "Put a cork in the gory details, will you?"

Once Jema emptied her stomach, Diana took her down the hall to tidy up. That gave Cailean the chance to speak freely to the McDonnels about her and her brother.

"Master, did you read her aura?" When Bhaltair nodded he said to the laird, "Jema McShane is no' completely druid kind. She carries the blood of other magic folk in her veins. Since her brother is a twin, so must he."

"What difference does that make?" Kinley asked. "They had enough druid blood to cross over to us."

"Mixing the blood of two different magic races produces children of a peculiar nature," Bhaltair said. "Some are affected physically. Others grow very powerful."

"The Skaraven were both," Lachlan said. At Kinley's quizzical look he added, "They were an ancient race of Pritani warriors, purposely bred from two different tribes of magic folk to be bigger, stronger and faster than ordinary men."

His wife grimaced. "I bet that worked out well."

"'Tis said that they were as unstoppable as berserkers, and twice as frightening," Raen said, and regarded Bhaltair. "The first druids had a hand in creating the Skaraven, did they no', Master Flen?"

The old man snorted. "I am no' so old as that, Seneschal."

Cailean admired how deftly his master dismissed what had been a disastrous time for their people. In reality the Skaraven had been ever more terrifying than their legend maintained.

Diana returned with Jema, who tried to retreat to a corner. Bhaltair stepped into her path and said, "Mistress McShane, would you permit me to read your bloodline? 'Twillnae harm you, and we may learn much from its revelations."

Jema looked at the laird. "If I do this, will you release Tormod, and help me find Gavin?"

"We shall send a warband to track and recover your twin, Mistress McShane," Lachlan said, looking grim now. "The Viking violated an oath he gave of his own accord. I cannae pardon him for breaking his pledge to me, as it doesnae respect all the other men who hold to it."

She stared at the floor and said nothing for a long moment. "All right, I'll do as you ask."

Bhaltair gestured for her to sit, and took the opposite chair before he held out his gnarled hands. "If you will place your palms atop mine, Mistress." Once she had, he folded his fingers over hers, and his eyes took on a faint shimmer of power.

Cailean stood behind his master and added his power to that of Bhaltair's. The old druid murmured the spell and it materialized in the air between him and Jema. Two images coalesced almost instantaneously.

"Anea Fhost, druidess healer of the Stone Feather people, shares your bloodline," Bhaltair murmured, nodding at the glowing female figure. "As does Eryk Fire Blade, Norrvegr raider."

Cailean sent his thoughts through the connection to Bhaltair's spell and read the past lives of Jema's ancestors. "Anea was a powerful herbalist who came upon Eryk as he lay dying," the ovate said. "She took pity and had him brought to her home, where she cared for his burns. As she brought him back from the edge of death, they fell in love.

Although Eryk was a shaman, and as powerful as she in his own right, they both knew he would never be accepted by Anea's people. Since his tribe had been wiped out, they left her village. They joined a settlement of renegades like them in the islands, where they lived out their lives in peace."

Bhaltair blinked and regarded the two figures hovering in the air before he muttered a phrase and they disappeared. "The child of a druidess healer and a shamanic warrior." He met Jema's wide-eyed gaze. "You have a foot in the magic of two worlds, Mistress McShane. You are Viking as well as druid kind."

"It also explains her brother's behavior toward the female undead," Cailean said. "He is likely too powerful for her to bring him entirely under her sway. We must be very cautious with how we manage him."

"My brother isn't powerful. He was dying of a terminal disease in my time." Jema jerked to her feet. "Even if crossing over healed him, as you've told me, he's lost and alone and confused. He's been enslaved by a woman who drinks blood. How can you talk about him like he's an enemy?"

"And I think we've had enough druid chit chat for one night," Diana said and touched Jema's shoulder. "Come on, sweetheart. You need a break from all this." She looked over at Raen. "I'll stay with her. She can spend the night in the old guest room. We'll get moving on the rescue op in the morning, okay?"

Her husband didn't look happy, but he nodded, and Diana guided the distraught woman out of the map room.

❧

JEMA FELT numb as she accompanied Diana down the passage to a set of stairs that led down several levels. She should never have revealed herself to Rachel. If she'd just stayed cloaked Tormod wouldn't be locked in a dungeon now. Somehow she had to shift the blame for this mess away from him, and convince the laird that it had been all her fault.

As the air grew steamy Jema emerged from her misery to look around them, and then stared at Diana. "There aren't any guest rooms by the cistern chambers."

"No, but there is a back way into the dungeon. Took me forever to find it, too." Diana ducked into a narrow passage, and motioned for Jema to stay back as she eased open a creaky door. She peeked inside. "We're in luck. Evander hasn't sent a guard to watch him yet. Come on."

Jema slipped through the doorway after the redhead, and walked as quietly as she could through a room crowded with medieval instruments of torture, all of which sat dust-covered and cobwebbed from lack of use.

"We don't actually torture anyone, by the way," Diana said as she stepped in front of a barred cell, and planted her hands on her hips. "But I'm making a recommendation that we start with this one."

"It took you long enough to find me," Tormod said. He was stretched out on a cot, but sat up and grinned at Jema. "But you brought a present for me. I forgive you now."

"I don't understand," Jema said as Tormod rose to his feet, and Diana took out a set of old iron keys. "You two planned this?"

"Ah, despite his bullshit in the great hall, the dumbass never plans anything," the redhead told her as she opened the cell door. "I, on the other hand, am prepared for everything."

Jema flew into Tormod's arms, and he held her and kissed every part of her face he could reach as she laughed with relief.

"Now I can give you this." He took out the map disc, which he had polished and hung from a fine silver chain. He draped it around her neck. "'Tis all that came with you and I dinnae want you to lose it."

She touched the gleaming silver and now knew it had to have come from the dig. "It's beautiful."

"Look, you two. I love a desperate romantic reunion as much as the next gal, but in about thirty minutes my husband is going to stop by the real guest room. Actually, he'll probably want to swap me out for a guard so he doesn't have to sleep alone because he's a big baby that way. And as soon as he sees we're not there, he'll come running here." Diana handed Tormod a heavily-stuffed purse and a small scroll case. "The village where they were last seen is called Dovebart, and I've marked it on the map. Go out through the cistern. You want to head due north. They'll hit the ocean about twenty miles west of the sea stacks."

Tormod hustled Jema out of the cell, and then turned with a frown as Diana locked herself inside and tossed him the keys. "What do you now, you mad wench?" he demanded as he caught them.

"Oh, I brought Jema down here to give you a good-night kiss, and the two of you jumped me. I think that's why she insisted on it. You obviously knew what the laird was going to do to you, because you gave her the keys to your cell in advance." She stretched out on the pallet and folded her arms behind her head. "You also stole Meg's kitchen funds to finance your escape. By the time they find me you should be who knows where, you treacherous thief." She tapped her lips. "Did I actually just use the word treacherous in a real sentence?"

The Viking muttered something vile under his breath.

"I adore you, too, you sneaky bastard."

She winked at Jema. "Take care of him for me, okay?"

Tormod took Jema by the hand and guided her back to the cistern level, where he kissed her again before he said, "I'll tell you everything once we're safe. For now you must trust me."

She nodded, and then yelped as he scooped her up against him.

"Close your eyes, and when I say, hold your breath." He waded into the old cistern pool up to his waist. "Now."

Jema sank down into the steaming water with him, her body suddenly immersed in streams of bubbles. She felt light pressing against her eyelids, and then suddenly she was being pulled through the water, which went from hot to icy cold. Keeping her eyes closed took all of her nerve, but just as her lungs began to ache for air she surfaced with Tormod, and gasped.

"Look now," he encouraged her, and when she opened her eyes he swam with her to a nearby mossy bank.

Somehow they had gone from the cistern chamber to a slow-moving river in the highlands. Jema thought she might be hallucinating until she saw the dark silhouette of a cow looking at them from behind a rickety fence.

Tormod brushed a lock of wet hair from her face. "You've got back your memory."

"Aye, I have." She rubbed her cheek against his hand before she flopped back and stared up at the trees. "My name is Jema McShane, and I am not married or promised to anyone. As I suspected, I have no children. I search for the past by digging holes in the ground, and studying very old things other people find."

"You mean that you're an archaeologist." When she uttered a startled laugh he helped her to stand and looked a little smug. "Red is very fond of one of your kind, a man named Jones. She told me of his adventures one morning after our run. He mustnae be a handsome man, to forever be chasing treasure instead of wenches. And what manner of given name is Indiana?"

Jema wondered if she could adequately explain the concept of a movie to him. "We'll discuss that another time. I don't chase after treasure, but I do look for history. I've been working a dig in the Scottish highlands looking for a Viking artifact: a golden diamond called Freyja's Eye."

Tormod's amusement vanished. "Why would you wish to find that facking cursed rock?"

"To prove that it actually exists, and become very famous, and land a better job so I can pay for my brother's care." She explained about Gavin's ALS, and how teaching at Edinburgh would enable her to provide him with the best medical treatment available. "I thought it might be buried with the Viking warrior, but before I could finish excavating the grave something happened. Gavin and I fell in the trench, and crossed over to your time."

She bunched up some of her shirt and squeezed water from it as he did the same.

"The portal will have healed your brother. To take him back to your time will cause him to become afflicted again. Aye, 'twas what happened to Diana when she was forced to return. The tumor in her head grew back, and caused her to have a…stroke?" He glanced at her, and when she nodded he said, "She was dying in the hospital when Kinley, Raen and I went to the future to fetch her."

She stopped what she was doing. "Then Gavin can't go back," she whispered.

Despite her sodden, icy clothes Jema felt suddenly and inexplicably hot—the same kind of heat when she'd encountered the Aesir.

"Do you feel that?" she said and reached out to take Tormod's hand.

The heat flooded along her arm into his, and steam began to rise from their bodies. When she snatched her hand back their clothes were warm and completely dry.

"I'm sorry," Jema said quickly. "I didn't mean to do that."

"I'm no'. Heat me up whenever you wish, lass." Tormod took out the scroll case Diana had given to him, and removed from it a very detailed, beautifully drawn map. He traced a short length on a swirling line, and tapped a cluster of triangles. "We'll follow the river here, to Dovebart." Without warning, he pulled his tunic back from his shoulder. "Ah, fack me."

His ink lit up and began to spin, while the

arrow on her forearm shimmered as it darted back and forth over her flesh. Jema felt the map disc grow hot against her breast, and quickly tugged the chain off over her head. The lines etched on the silver pendant glowed with white light, which reflected on Tormod's map as a series of circles and arrows leading past the village to the north coast. Beyond the shore an oval briefly appeared, reflected from a tiny golden shard embedded in the center of the disc.

"I know this spot," Jema murmured as she studied the light tracings on the map. "This is where the Picts tried to stop a Viking invasion. According to the sagas, there was a terrible battle at sea just beyond a small island that neither side won."

"Aye, in the end all the ships went to the bottom," Tormod said. "Every warrior drowned, and the place was cursed. Even now merchant ships give the skerry a wide berth when they sail through those waters."

The light on the disc gradually disappeared, and their tattoos stopped moving. Jema exhaled with relief. Then she saw how grim his expression had grown. "What is it?"

"The Viking invasion was led by a shield-maiden named Thora the Merciless," he told her. "She alone survived the battle. 'Twas said Freyja's Eye protected her by sinking the enemy ships."

"Her name was Thora?"

He nodded. "She was my sister."

Thora the Merciless had lived at the end of the first century, over twelve hundred years before Tormod's time. "But that's not possible."

"'Tis a story for another time." He rolled up the map and stuffed it back in the case. "We must speak to the mortals who might have seen your brother."

Jema thought of all the other times Tormod had referred to people as mortals. He had a sister who had been born twelve centuries before him. She also knew no ordinary man could use bodies of water like his own personal tube.

"You're not mortal, are you?"

Tormod looked up at the night sky, shook his head, and put his arm around her shoulders. "I've broken my oath to the laird, so 'twill no' hurt to tell you. What I say now, you cannae repeat to anyone, even your brother. Give me your word, lass."

"Of course, I promise I won't say anything." She started to feel a little alarmed. "Is it that bad?"

"I cannae name it bad or good," he admitted, and guided her up to an old path leading away from the river. "'Tis what 'twas."

As they walked toward the village, Tormod described his tribe leaving Norway for the Isle of Skye, where they built a small settlement. "Our jarl didnae realize the island had been claimed by the Pritani long before we arrived."

Tormod spoke of how his tribe had prospered on Skye, and when the clashes had begun with the Pritani. Their arrogant jarl had decided to claim the entire island, and sent a messenger to tell the Pritani they had to leave. No reply came, and the messenger was never seen again.

"Our finest warriors were sent into the mountains to attack the Pritani," he said as he helped her over the vine-covered log of a fallen tree. "They found the village deserted, and set fire to it. When the men returned they declared it a great victory. The Pritani had fled Skye, they said, and the island was ours. They didnae know that our enemy had gone to a sacred place on the island to bury their chieftain, who had just died. The new chieftain had wanted to make peace with us, but there was no greater insult than to inflict violence on those in grief."

Jema cringed. "Oh, no."

"That night our men drank, and our women danced," he said softly. "All the while the Pritani waited and watched from the shadows. At dawn the next day, they put our village to the torch. My mother bade me take my sister to my father's dory, and leave the island. Later I learned that my mother died with my father, trying to save our stock from burning."

Jema tugged him to a stop, and put her arms around him. "My parents died together, and without Gavin I might not have survived it. I'm so sorry, Tormod."

He held her close for a time, and then drew back. "I did save Thora, but only by distracting the Pritani long enough for her to run to the boat. I was captured and made a slave, but my sister escaped. Ten more years would pass before the Romans came to Scotland hunting the druids. When the Pritani tribes all came together to fight for the magic folk, my master allowed me to stand with them."

Jema frowned. "I don't understand. The Romans came to Scotland in the first century. That was…twelve hundred years before this time."

"Aye. Twelve centuries past, we were killed by the Romans. They threw our bodies into Loch Sìorraidh, where we lay until the magic folk worked a mighty spell, and brought us back to life." He gently nudged her jaw so that her mouth closed. "The druids took vengeance for our slaying by casting our deaths on the legion. We became immortals, and they were made undead blood-drinkers. We've been at war ever since."

Hot tears blurred her vision. "You're twelve hundred years old?"

"And more. I was a man when the Romans ended me." He rubbed her shoulders with a soothing caress. "'Twas how I wished to die, as a fighting warrior. I thought Freyja would choose me from the slain to join her guard, as

I was the only Viking among the dead. She wouldnae wish the Pritani to spend eternity protecting Asgard and the Aesir."

"But instead you joined the McDonnel clan," she said quietly. He was either the most forgiving man she'd ever known, or the craziest. "After what they did to you and your tribe, how could you bare it?"

"My slavery allowed my sister to be free. I wasnae treated badly, and my people had burned their village first. I wanted my life to have meaning, and that the Pritani gave it." He saw her reaction and smiled a little. "What we endured at the hands of the Romans saved the magic folk. Awakening together as immortals made us brothers." His mouth hitched. "I havenae a drop of Scots blood, but I chose to make the clan my family. I dinnae regret it."

That reminded her. "You were half-right about my ancestors," Jema said. "Master Flen performed a spell to read my bloodline. It seems that I'm descended from an illicit love affair between a druid herbalist, and a Viking shaman named Eryk Fire Blade."

His brows arched high. "Eryk Fire Blade was our shaman. I thought him killed in the burning." Tormod smiled. "'Tis good to learn he survived it, and found a new life with his druidess."

"You know what that means." Though the connection might be a coincidence, it still made Jema shiver. "You *are* my tribe."

"Aye, there's no avoiding it, lass." He kissed her brow. "Now we'll go and get back our brother."

## Chapter Fourteen

THORA FELT THE unfamiliar gnaw of hunger, and reined in her mount as she took in the landscape. Returning to Midgard had come with the uncomfortable price of occupying the form of a blood-drinker, but she paid it without complaint. There was much to admire about her new form. Its strength and speed were far superior to what her own had been in mortal life.

Gavin guided his horse alongside hers. "The sun will rise soon. We have to find shelter."

Thora nodded, her eyes narrowing as she spotted the cultivated fields of a small farm.

"There," she said, pointing at the neat rows of ripe oats. "The house will have a cellar or store room where I may rest."

"And you must feed," Gavin said.

Thora's insides shriveled. She knew from Fenella's memories what her life would have to be like. But where Fenella relished feeding on the life-blood of mortals, it revolted Thora. Her jaw tightened but at last she nodded and rode with Gavin to the property.

The farm boasted a house and barn, and from the look of the penned livestock enjoyed much prosperity. Thora didn't wait for Gavin to help her dismount but vaulted off, her cold body suddenly thrumming with hunger. She watched a thin, haggard-looking male emerge from the house, a cudgel in one hand and a dagger in the other.

"What do ye want?" the mortal demanded.

"My lady is weary, and there are no lodgings for miles," Gavin said in a thicker version of his own accent. "We can pay for a room."

The farmer cursed him and headed back inside, coming up short when Thora intercepted him. "Ye cannot stay here," he whined. "We've death in the house."

"I'm afraid we must," she said and swatted the weapons from his hands. The pulse of the old man's jugular quickened and she stared hard at it, licking her lips.

"Thora," Gavin said, his tone stern and warning. She forced herself to look at him. "If you want blood, you can drink mine." He gestured toward the house. "Go inside while I tie him up in the barn."

"*Blood?*" the old man gasped, trying to back up, but Gavin grabbed him, easily picking him up, and headed toward the barn.

*Yes, blood*, Thora thought grimly as she watched them go. Only when they had disappeared could she make herself turn away.

Inside the farm house Thora saw a shrouded body in a crude coffin, and a second, much smaller bundle tucked in a basket. The scent of old blood painted the air, and when she tugged down the edge of the shroud she saw the lifeless features of a young mortal female. When she unwrapped the bundle in the basket she found a dead fetus no bigger than the palm of her hand. She pulled back the shroud over the mother and tucked the dead infant against her breast.

"You should have chosen another life than this." She heard the front door close.

"Is that why you became a warrior?" Gavin asked as he joined her. "You feared childbirth?"

Thora fixed him with gaze. "I fear naught, McShane. I became a shield-maiden so I might kill with my own hands the Pritani scum who murdered my tribe, my parents and my brother. I couldnae see it done as a mortal. 'Tis been twelve centuries since my death, but with the help of Freyja's Eye I will soon see justice done."

Gavin gave the dead woman and child a long, sorrowful look before he covered their bodies.

"I see no sign of a cellar," he told her, "but they've a bed chamber without windows."

Thora followed him into the adjoining room, her fangs stretching out painfully into her mouth. The hunger that coursed through every fiber of her was threatening to sweep away reason. But when Gavin turned to her she saw him plying his blade against his wrist.

"As I promised," he told her and offered her his arm.

Thora inhaled sharply as the coppery scent of his blood filled her nostrils. Though she tried not to hurry, she gripped his powerful forearm and placed her cold mouth on his warm flesh. She drank from the wound, but only enough to stop the ache of the hunger. Then as Fenella would have done, she used a drop of her blood to heal the cut, and met his gaze. They had never stood so close and for the first time since she'd met him she felt as though she actually saw him. Perhaps the hunger had clouded her mind more than she'd known, but Gavin McShane had gray-blue eyes the color of the winter sea. His rugged features matched his massively muscled body, which all but glowed with the vibrance of a life that was now forever lost to her.

His eyes searched hers now, then drifted down to her lips. For a moment his gaze lingered there and she wondered if there was blood. Quickly she swiped the back of her hand across her mouth, but there had been no blood. She looked at him quizzically, only to find that his broad hand now cupped the side of her face.

"You were beautiful in form and figure before, but now..." He gently wrapped his arm around her and brought their faces close. She could feel his warm breath on her lips. "Now you are more lovely than a pale goddess of the moon, and I see the sunset in your eyes." He touched his lips to hers.

Thora had never kissed anyone. Her mortal kin had avoided the practice, and among her raiders it would have been decidedly reckless to show such preference for any man. But Gavin was not any man. Fenella had once enthralled him, but Thora knew that was ended. He was responding to something more than the prefect's body. And she found that her mouth was responding to his.

He gathered her against him and she could feel the long bulge of his manhood, stiff with desire. He meant to fack her, and that made an odd pleasure rise up in her. She had coupled with some of her fellow warriors, mainly to work off nerves before a battle.

Fenella, on the other hand, had loved facking.

The blood-drinker's memories of romping stretched far back into her mortal life, when she had eagerly spread her legs for the comely cowherds and pretty milk maids at the dairy. She would lay down with anyone willing to kiss and touch and penetrate her, it seemed. Once enthralled by Quintus Seneca, Fenella had happily whored herself for her undead master. Since being turned and made prefect, however, Fenella had devoted herself to facking and then murdering her partners, mostly enthralled mortals but several undead Romans as well.

Though Thora abhorred the prefect's penchant for killing sex, Fenella's endless lust seemed to be infecting her. She slipped her hand between the press of their bodies, and freed Gavin's rampant cock. Another tug and she opened her trews, dropping them out of the way. Gavin moved her backward toward the bed and when she fell on it, he removed her trews, then pulled her shirt and vest off over her head. He ripped off his own clothes, revealing his magnificent male body, before he came over her.

"Thora," he ground out through a clenched jaw, "say now if I must stop."

In response, her cold fingers explored the hard ridges of his stomach and chest. "Put yourself inside me," she whispered.

He fisted his shaft and brought his thick cockhead to her opening.

Thora stared up into his fierce eyes as the hot, broad head of his shaft pressed into her cool sex. The heat of him spread through her belly, awakening new desires. The stretching sensations of her gloving him sent a jolt of excitement that she felt in her fangs.

Gavin's jaw tightened as he went deeper, and he gripped her shoulders once he'd filled her completely. "I knew you'd feel like heaven around me." Carefully he drew out of her, and then forged back inside, the slick friction making her gasp. "Oh, aye, there, now you feel it, don't you? I'm inside you, Thora. I'm loving you."

He thrust again, faster and harder, making the bed shake from the pumping force.

Suddenly her breasts came to painful life, and puckered at their tips until they felt like pebbles. That had never happened to her.

"How can this be?" she gasped.

"It's what you need," he breathed. "It makes you feel everything you've forgotten from your life. It makes you alive again. It makes you mine, Thora."

Gavin never looked away from her face as he fucked her, his deep, hard shafting fueling the desperate ache inside her. Thora was astonished over the climax building inside her, but the delight soon threatened to swamp her.

"But I'm no' a mortal," she said, her voice trembling as she thrashed under him, battling this new hunger within, even as he plowed into her with more passion.

"You will come, my sweet lass."

Gavin bent his dark head to her small breasts, fastening his mouth on one nipple to suck it with firm, deep tugs. He lifted his head only to do the same to her other mound before he reached down to draw her legs up and drag her hips down to the very edge of the bed.

He stood on the floor, and gripped her hips as he pounded into her. As his thrusts grew faster, it felt as if his hard, thick cock had turned into a blunt iron sword. Soon Thora cried out and shook all over as the burning pleasure inside her threatened to burst and shatter her into pieces.

It was at that moment that Gavin drove deep and clamped her nipples between his fingers, pinching them gently as he said, "Let go, sweetheart. Let go and give yourself to me. I'll never betray you, Thora. I'll always be your man."

A dam hidden inside Thora gave way as the pleasure poured through her, sweeping away everything but the delight of Gavin mastering her senses as well as her body. Dimly she heard him groan, and felt the spurting warmth of his seed bathing her clenching insides. It pushed her through that orgasm and into another, and she shook helplessly in his arms, her body contracting tightly around him. She felt his shaft hardening again inside her, and Gavin made a strange sound.

Thora moaned softly as she felt him jet inside her a second time.

"I've not been with a woman for years," Gavin gasped as he withdrew and fell beside her. "You make me come like I'll never stop."

"Imagine if 'twas centuries, McShane," she chided, snuggling up against him.

Thora held him as their bodies cooled and relaxed. She stared up at the tightly-thatched ceiling, her sex sated but her fangs throbbing anew with hunger. But she lay with him until he had fallen deep into slumber. Then silently she rose from the bed, dressed, and went to the barn. In the back she found the farmer dozing atop some grain sacks, his wrists and ankles bound by rope.

He stirred as she knelt down beside him, and then cowered as soon as he opened his eyes. "No, dinnae touch me."

"I wish I didnae need to," she said, thrusting his head back as she bit his neck.

Unlike with Gavin, she drank her fill. But it wasn't just her blood-hunger that needed to be satisfied. Fenella's memories had found a way to deliver Thora's vengeance more quickly. She looked down at the marks she had left in his neck. Thora bit her finger and ran it over the wound.

As soon as the punctures closed the farmer's expression grew bright with joy. "How may I serve you, my sweet lady?"

Thora smiled but without joy. "You will take a horse and journey west to the Isle of Skye."

"What do ye wish me to do on Skye?" the farmer asked.

"There is a man you must find and reward for me. His name is McDonnel."

## Chapter Fifteen

DIANA LOOKED UP from her *gomukhasana* as her husband unlocked her dungeon cell, and began to unwind herself from the yoga pose. "Hey, sweet." She released the handhold behind her back and untwisted her entwined legs. "I wasn't expecting conjugal visits when Evander threw me in here."

Raen's gray eyes looked almost black as he regarded her. "You put yourself in there, Wife. Twice." He reached down and helped her to her feet. "We're leaving."

She feigned shock. "You mean we got kicked out of the clan, too? Holy crap. Does that mean we have to go live with Grandpa Bhaltair and his merry band of druids?"

"No. We've formed a warband to go after Tormod and Jema. You'll be our tracker." When she would have replied he shook his head. "You'll track the facking Viking, and naught else."

"No, I'm just not interested." She dropped back down onto the floor and stretched out her long legs. "You can go. Unless you want to have dirty dungeon sex with me, in which case, baby, bring me some shackles."

"Diana, we need your help," Lachlan said. He came around Raen to look at her. "I am persuaded no' to punish Tormod for concealing the woman, but we must find them before they run afoul of Fenella Ivar. You ken how dangerous she is."

Diana blushed, and pinched the bridge of her nose for a moment to cover it. "Two conditions: you kill Fenella so this girl's brother doesn't become an undead lackey." When the laird nodded she said, "And you forget what you just heard me say to Raen about the dungeon sex. Immediately. Please."

The laird grinned. "Done and done." He glanced at her husband before he added, "We leave within the hour."

Diana cradled her knees as she watched Lachlan depart, and then looked up at her very unhappy highlander. "You can yell at me, you know. I did bad things for a good reason."

Raen made a nasty sound, and looked around the cell. "For Tormod, you did this. Tormod, who isnae your husband. If you forget, I am."

She'd been expecting this conversation for a while, so it wasn't entirely rattling her. She just wasn't sure if someone as well-liked as her husband could understand it. Better that she start out simple, Diana decided.

"He's like my brother, Big Man. That's all. There's nothing going on between the two of us."

Raen muttered to himself in Pritani as he paced back and forth outside her cell. Occasionally he also slammed his fist into something unbreakable. Diana watched him, feeling just a little worried now. One of the main reasons Raen never held a grudge was because he was basically invincible. If he fought another man in earnest, he wasn't going to lose.

Finally he came into the cell and crouched

down in front of her. "You're my wife, no' his. Your loyalty belongs to me."

"I think he's in love with Jema," she said. "While I'm in love with you. But I'm loyal to whoever I choose. Actually I'm kind of flexible on loyalty. Whoever earns it at the moment, gets it."

Raen rocked back onto his heels. "I dinnae understand this bond between you and the Viking, but I havenae challenged it. After what you've said and done, Diana, I begin to think that I should."

"Now that Scotty's here I don't think you'll have to." She smiled sadly. "Before Jema he had no one. He isn't even Pritani. He's surly and makes trouble and generally acts like an ass to get attention. To have you see him. Because otherwise, unless they have work for him to do, everyone ignores him."

Raen blinked. "What?"

"Before I came here I don't think Tormod ever had a friend." She rested the back of her head against the wall. "He has no tribe. He's not Pritani. He was a slave for ten years. I mean, honestly, what McDonnel is going to want him as a bestie?"

"He chose to join the clan after the awakening," her husband snapped. "He wasnae forced to."

"I can't believe he did it, either," Diana said. "He watched Lachlan's tribe murder his people and burn his village to the ground, and then he was captured and enslaved by them. When the Pritani finally freed him, it was only to fight the damn Romans, who then butchered him. Then he wakes up an immortal with no one but the clan. What the hell did you expect him to do?"

Raen grimaced. "Gods, Diana, when you say it so…"

"Yeah, well, it is what it is, right?" She crawled into his lap. "Look, the Viking and I are both orphans. As kids we had no one to love us. I was abandoned as an infant, and beaten and nearly starved to death in foster care. Of course we were going to bond."

He stroked his big hand over her hair. "Forgive me. I love you so much, sometimes I think I will go mad with it."

"You weren't entirely off the mark," she said, looking up into his rugged face. "Tormod was falling in love with me, I think, when I chose you. What's amazing is that he wasn't jealous or upset about it. He wants me to be happy. I want the same thing for him. So." She plucked a piece of lint off his vest. "I'll always love him, and protect him, but I can only ever be like a sister to Tormod. Because you're my guy, and my heart belongs to you."

He kissed her, long and slow, and released her only when she was shaking and clutching at him. "We dinnae have time for dirty dungeon sex, or you *would* be in shackles."

Leaving the dungeon and rejoining the clan upstairs did give Diana a sense of relief. She hadn't demolished her marriage or her relationship with the laird. While Evander still gave her the stink eye as soon as he saw her, he would come around, once he remembered that they shared the Talorc bloodline, and her awesome tracking powers often came in handy.

*Or not,* Diana thought as she smiled at her cousin, *and I'll have to watch my back for the rest of eternity.*

Bhaltair appeared by her side. "I should have you disciplined by the conclave," he murmured as the laird explained their mission to the other members of the warband. "Their punishments are quite unpleasant. They might even disincarnate you."

"Nice try, but no sale, Grandpa." Diana muttered back. "I share a soul with my husband. Punish me, you punish him."

"I shall still scold you at the very next opportunity," the old druid promised. "At length. Harshly."

Diana was assigned to track the Viking and his lady from Dovebart to the coast, where what they found would decide how they would continue the mission.

Kinley became very grumpy about being left out, but she agreed that with her status and ability to throw fire she was the logical choice to remain behind to safeguard the stronghold. She still walked out to the loch with her husband, and wished the rest of the party good luck.

"Don't get into it with Tormod," Kinley told Evander. "Save it for the lists."

"As you say, my lady," the captain agreed thinly.

"I know how you feel. Leaving me behind

will keep Tormod from having his ass burned to a crisp."

The sound of a horn from the curtain wall drew everyone's attention. Near the tower a guard was pointing to the stronghold's narrow approach.

"Single rider!" he shouted.

Before Diana had a chance to react, Raen and Evander were sprinting to the road. Lachlan moved Kinley and Rachel back to where Diana and the druids stood, then placed himself in front of them. More warriors poured through the gate and formed a line of shields in front of the laird that bristled with swords.

The rider was thin and wild-eyed, waving a bloody dirk above his head.

"The laird must die," he called out in a shrill voice. "The Mistress bade me cut his neck."

"Enthralled," Rachel said to Diana. "But how did he know to come here?"

Diana's stomach took a dive. One of the clan's most important secrets was the location of Dun Aran. They'd managed to conceal it since becoming immortals. If the undead had finally discovered how to find them…

"Rachel," Kinley said, "you need to read him and find out everything he knows."

"Agreed," Diana said, stepping forward with her.

Without turning, Lachlan held out his giant arm to block their way. "You'll stay where you are," he said, his voice low but with a tone that said he should not be disobeyed.

"Who is your Mistress?" Raen called out.

Twenty yards away the man had reined in his horse, yet swayed in the saddle as though the mare still moved. "Where is McDonnel?" he shrieked. "I am for him and him alone!"

Lachlan stepped forward, approaching Raen and Evander who stood shoulder to shoulder, their weapons at the ready.

"I am Lachlan, laird of the McDonnels. Have your say."

"You didnae kill all of them," the mortal screamed, almost giddy. "She got away. She has never forgot. You will die." His eyes bulged and rolled as he looked at the rest of the warband, and grinned. "You shall all burn."

With a nimbleness belied by his erratic movements, the wild man twisted and hurled the blood-stained dirk at Lachlan.

"No!" Kinley screamed.

But in an instant, Raen's blade flashed through the air, cleaving the dagger in two. The useless pieces flew in different directions, one landing in the loch.

Simultaneously Evander flung his short spear. It rammed through the mortal's chest, dislodging him from the saddle, and sent him sailing backward off his mount.

"Wait!" Rachel cried.

She made an anguished sound and raced past the men, as Diana and Kinley followed. Though blood already ran in small rivulets over the ground, Rachel bent to the impaled man and touched his arm. Her lips whitened, but she didn't stop focusing on him until the last breath wheezed from his lungs.

Evander helped her stand and put an arm around her as she swayed. "You shouldnae have done that, my love."

"I know," she said, sounding tired. She regarded the laird. "His name was Thomas, and he had a farm near Dovebart. His wife just died in childbirth, along with the baby." She swiped at her brimming eyes. "The woman who used him for blood and sent him here to kill you is not Fenella Ivar. Her name is Thora Liefson, and she died at the end of the first century. Her spirit has possessed the undead woman."

"Tormod's sister was named Thora," Diana said, drawing everyone's attention. "He's been trying to find her grave so he could bring her back here and bury her with his parents." She turned to Bhaltair as he joined them. "If she was Viking, how could she possess anyone?"

"I am no' a Norseman, so I cannae tell you that," the old druid admitted. "My lady Talorc, did you glean from this poor soul why Thora Liefson sent him to attack the laird, and how she knew the castle was here?"

"In my mortal life," Lachlan said before Rachel could answer, "my tribe's village was burned down by hers, and we retaliated. The stronghold is built on the ashes of my old village. She wasnae attacking the laird of the McDonnels. She was trying to kill the Pritani warmaster who slaughtered her tribe."

Raen looked stricken. "Tormod's sister was Thora the Merciless?"

"She is," Rachel gently corrected. "She's returned to life to finish her quest. Thora Liefson intends to kill every last Pritani that is still alive." She nodded to the laird. "That would be you and every member of this clan, my lord."

"She's but one woman," Evander chided gently. "What can she do, even with the help of Jema's brother?"

"The same that she did to all of the Pritani warships," Raen said. "My lord, I think Thora Liefson goes to retrieve Freyja's Eye."

## Chapter Sixteen

AFTER LEARNING FROM the villagers in Dovebart that Fenella and Gavin had stolen two horses, Tormod decided to water-travel to the coast to get ahead of them. As he led Jema to the edge of a forest stream out of sight of the village, she hesitated at the edge as he waded in.

"You've done this twice now, my lass," he told her, holding out his hand. "Dinnae be afraid of it a third."

She smiled at him. "I'm not. I just can't imagine you joining with water, or becoming one with the water. I'm still not sure what you mean. Maybe I should just see it first."

He lifted her down into the rushing current and let his bond with the element transform him into his traveling form. "And now?"

Jema's jaw sagged. He knew what she saw. Though his body still held its natural shape, it was water. She touched his transparent cheek, gasping when her fingers sank into his face.

"It turns you *into* water?"

"In some ways, aye. In others I'm still a man. 'Tis another of the clan's secrets." He curled his arms around her. "You might keep your eyes open, but hold your breath still, and dinnae let go of me."

They submerged and the stream illuminated and began to bubble around them as he thought of a river that emptied into the sea. For him moving through the water was as simple as breathing, but he kept a close eye on his lady to assure she was not too frightened. A few moments later they surfaced, and he carried her out of the water to stand and watch it pour over a cliff.

"*Losh*," she exclaimed and looked down at the falls crashing against the cliff base. "What happens if you're pulled over?"

He dragged his wet hair back from his face. "I stay in my traveling form, lass, so I dinnae break all my bones when I land." He squinted at her. "You would not fare as well."

"I'll remember that," Jema said, backing away from the edge. "So how far are we from Dovebart?"

"Fifteen leagues or so," he said and eyed the horizon. "There's a town past that curve in the shore. There we'll find rooms, and wait for Fenella and your brother to show."

Jema rested her hands against his chest, once more drying their garments with the heat from her ink, and then glanced down at herself. "I should have changed into clothes from your time. I'd better cloak myself until we're out of sight."

In town Tormod found an inn that overlooked the water, and roused the sleepy innkeeper, who agreed to lodge him for a few coins. "I've been traveling all night," he told the stout man. "Let me sleep the day."

The innkeeper tapped his brow and yawned as he retreated down the stairs.

Opening the door, Tormod waited a moment and then moved inside, shutting the door as Jema uncloaked herself.

"Oh, I'd kill to have a camera and a

laptop," she murmured as she made a circuit of the room to examine the lamps and furnishings. "We always assumed medieval inns were filthy, flea-ridden flop houses."

Tormod glanced around the tidy room. "Why would anyone pay coin for that when they could simply stay home?"

Though she smiled, her mood sobered when she stood at the window to look down at the docks. "Do you really think they'll come here?"

"I cannae swear it, but the map disc and our ink sent us to this place. Black ships have been seen before at these docks. Fenella has no idea that we are waiting for her." He went to stand with her and circled her waist with his arm. "We'll ken better when the sun sets."

"I can't take Gavin back with me to the future," she murmured. "I know he doesn't want to live with ALS anymore. Before he got sick he was a soldier. He can survive in your world."

"You might stay here with him." Tormod tugged her close to his side, and rubbed her shoulder. "Or I could go to the future with you."

"You'd give up your life here for me?" Before he could answer she made a face. "I forgot, you already have. Would you be happy in a world so different from your own?"

He turned her to face him, his arms fitting naturally around her waist. "I would be happy wherever and whenever you choose to be."

Again she smiled but only briefly. "If we do find Freyja's Eye, and it actually possesses the powers you say it does, I think it might have to go back to my time."

He grimaced. "'Twill bring you only misery, my sweet."

"Not if I put it in a museum."

She explained what the scholars of her time did with precious artifacts, and how their study of them helped them understand the distant past. As he listened Tormod knew she was speaking for his benefit, but even as she did, he couldn't understand it. He'd always suspected she had a brilliant mind, in the ways of the old and learned druids, and the Caledonian monks who created books from memory. Now hearing her speak of carbon dating and spectral analysis, he felt a heavy truth settle in his chest. He was too simple and brutish to ever share her life.

"You have gone very quiet," Jema murmured as she idly fingered the clasp on his vest. "I'll stop with all the endless academia."

"No, lass." He held her closer. "'Tis wondrous, what you ken. That you might learn so much. Mayhap the Eye would be safer in one of your universities or museums."

She reached up and gently traced the outline of his mouth, then looked into his eyes. "But…you don't want to go with me."

"I'm a fair map-maker, and a passable warrior," he said and kissed her fingers. "I can read and cipher and I know my numbers, but 'tis all I ken. A man like me doesnae have a place in a life like yours."

"Then I'll stay here with you," Jema said, patting his chest. "We'll find a way to safeguard the Eye, and work out things with the clan–"

"The clan is done with me, my lass." The sudden sorrow at the blunt admission surprised Tormod, for he had always felt like an outsider among the McDonnels. It was sobering to realize that they had become as much his family as Arn, Gilda and Thora. He saw Jema's miserable expression, and tried to make light of it. "Then again, the laird took back Evander, and he did much worse than hide a wench in his chambers. Now he is captain of the guard. For my wrongs mayhap the clan will make me chieftain."

"Or we could form a new clan with Gavin," she said. "I think we'll have to use my name, though."

"Clan McShane," Tormod said and thought about it for a moment. "Who shall be laird?

"You," she said with a little giggle. "Gavin hates to be in charge." Her gray-blue eyes sparkled with mirth and the hint of something else. "I'll have to take orders from you."

He grinned and bent his head to nuzzle below her ear. "Would you now?" His lips brushed over her fragrant skin. "I shall have to think on my first command."

She tilted her head to allow him access. "Hurry," she whispered.

As he smiled against the side of her neck, he led them next to the bed. "I ken it already." He cupped her bottom and brought her hips against his, pressing his swollen member to her. Though she gasped a little, she slowly responded by rubbing herself on him. "I'd have you naked on that bed."

Without a word, Jema stripped out of her clothes. Though he eyed every inch of her, he did the same. In moments he stripped back the bed covering and drew her down to lie next to him. But without prompting, Jema pressed her lips to the hollow between his collarbones, and trailed a line of soft kisses down the center of his chest. Bemused, Tormod watched her, and tightened his belly as she found his navel with her tongue. But when she shifted back, working herself between his legs and bracing her elbows on either side of his hips, he held his breath. He couldn't take his eyes off her as she wrapped her fingers around the base of his shaft, and stroked him with her other hand.

"A man can only imagine such things," he said hoarsely.

"Then it's time to dream," she said and touched her lips to the tight skin of his cock-head. The tip of her tongue flicked back and forth over its tiny eye.

Tormod's thighs tensed as he watched her work her mouth on him, first with her tongue and lips, and then taking him into the soft, warm wetness inside. The way she lightly sucked on him made his fists knot, and seeing her lips stretch around him sent such heat into his balls he had to look away to keep from coming.

For a time Jema toyed with him, licking and lashing his shaft with her tongue. Then, as if she could sense his burgeoning need, she took his cock in her mouth and slowly bobbed her head, pumping him in and out as if he were instead plowing her quim.

Tormod thought of what he would do to her, just as soon as she freed him from the everlasting, blissful greed of her lips. He would put his mouth to her breasts and bottom and pearl, and lick her until the pleasure made her scream.

He felt his balls tightening, and she must have as well, for she took him into her mouth as deeply as she could and held him there as she sucked his shaft with slow, firm pulls.

Tormod exploded with ecstasy, and then he was shooting into her mouth, his hips churning as he rode the path to bliss. She swallowed every spurt, and then let him slip from her lips as she rested her cheek against his hip.

He thanked the gods for his randy, tireless cock as he reached and lifted her onto his chest. Her quim, slick and hot, melted over his already swelling shaft. He nudged against her, seeking and finding the narrow gate to her garden. The brute in him wanted to skewer her until he felt her womb. The dreamer wished never to move another measure. He made peace with both by sinking into her, slow and smooth, feeling her softness glide against the distended veins and bulky girth until their nether hair meshed. Feeling her on him, clasping him, heating him and loving him made all his worries melt like frost at first light.

All the wenches he had ever lain with would not have known him now. The lusty romps he'd always enjoyed with them paled beside this slow, gentle dance with Jema. He marveled at the scent of her blending with his, and the feel of her soft skin against his tough hide. Spreading the curtain of her bright hair so that it veiled her shoulders made him imagine draping her in golden chains, or strings of pearls.

He had never spoken to any wench of his feelings. Even with Colblaith he had jested and laughed. With Diana he had hidden his heart. Now he understood why men and women waited so long to find the words, and the one deserving of them.

He said it against her lips, so that she would always remember it as part of a kiss. "Jema, I love you. Whatever you choose, and wherever you go, I shall follow. I dinnae wish to be in a world without you."

"Oh, Tormod," she gasped and clung to him, shaking as if fevered. "I've loved you for so long, and I thought I'd never be able to tell you. And now you love me. That is the world." She stiffened and cried out, her pleasure spilling over him as if wrought by their words of love.

True to his word, Tormod followed her.

They lay together in idyllic silence as the dawn came to pour light into the room.

"You should marry me," he mentioned, stroking her tousled bright hair. "I would make a fine husband, you ken. As long as you give me something to do, like make maps, or kill undead," he tacked on honestly. "Or any work you think would suit me."

Jema pillowed her head on his shoulder. "Well, I might cuff you to my bed and use you as my sex slave. You're very good at that. I'd feed you, of course, and let you get up every now and then for exercise. But other than that, it would be sex and sex and more sex. You'd never have to get dressed again."

Kissing her softly swollen lips, he said, "You should marry me *today*."

# Chapter Seventeen

GAVIN WOKE AT noon feeling tired and weak, but one look at his sleeping lady restored some of his strength. Thora's hair had gone almost completely dark, with only a few gilded streaks around her beautiful face. Drinking his blood had painted a blush of color on her pale cheeks, and reddened her soft lips. He pulled her close and held her until his own thirst drove him to his feet to look for water.

In the front room dust motes danced in the sunlight while he filled a cup from a water bucket by the hearth and drank. He grimaced at the smell of death rising from the bodies in the open coffin. He would have to bury the pair soon. It took ten cups to quench his thirst before he went into the barn to find the farmer gone. The ropes he'd used to restrain him sat atop some grain sacks. Little drops of blood stained the sacking material.

"*Thora*," he muttered. No wonder she had looked so sated.

Bitter disappointment filled him. Somehow he had convinced himself that their lovemaking had managed to change her. And maybe it had—but not enough. Thora would always be undead, and she would always need blood. Disappointment melded with anger. Though he was glad that Thora had returned to this world, he wouldn't wish such an existence on even a creature as vile as Fenella.

Rather than dwell on what could not be changed, Gavin found a shovel and picked a spot under an old oak, where he began digging the grave. With every heave of soil his foggy head cleared a little more. When she'd healed his wound last night he'd expected the enthrallment to return, but it hadn't. He'd been free of it since the moment Thora had possessed Fenella's body, and it seemed that was permanent.

An hour later Gavin climbed out of the

grave and dragged the coffin to it. Carefully he slid the wood box into the rough hole. He muttered the Lord's Prayer as he filled it with dirt, unwilling to bury the pair without something said over the grave.

Once he finished he leaned on the spade.

"I'm sorry for you and your baby," he said quietly. "I hope you'll be together in the next life."

He glanced at the house. It would be dark soon. He turned from the small pile of fresh dirt and headed for the barn. Washing in the icy water from the well there lifted the last of the fog from Gavin's brain. He couldn't allow Thora to keep feeding on him. Even when she tried to hold back she drank too much, and the blood loss would definitely kill him. Now he remembered what she'd said just before: she'd spoken of Freyja's Eye. Though the thought that it could be real should have been exciting, all it did was make him think of Jema.

*I could leave Thora and go back to the forest.*

There was a chance that Jema was out there somewhere, alive and looking for him. He ought to be looking for her. He didn't owe Thora anything. But even as he thought it, he knew it wasn't that simple. In fact it was a great deal more complicated than that now that he'd fallen in love with her.

Gavin walked into the house and rummaged through the kitchen until he found the makings of a cheese and jam sandwich. A cask of ale also tempted him, but with the blood loss he decided against imbibing. Eating filled the hole in his belly and gave him more energy. He went to check the barn for a bigger saddle to use on their remaining horse, which would have to carry them both on the final leg of their journey. He found the tack he wanted and brought it out to work on fitting it to the mount.

Washing up after adjusting the saddle, Gavin went in to check on Thora, who was just rousing. Once the twilight snuffed out the sun she stretched and climbed out of the bed to look through a trunk of the dead woman's clothes.

"Has the mortal returned?" Thora asked him as she tugged a linen shift over her head.

"No," he said, relieved that she wasn't going to lie to him. Even so he would have to guard his feelings. Though he felt sure that

Thora had been genuine with him while they made love, there was more to the returned Viking and her mission than he knew. “I put a bigger saddle on the last horse. We’ll have to ride together.”

She made a vague sound of agreement and sorted through some skirts. “We will wait to see if the mortal returns.”

Gavin wondered just what she’d ordered the man to do. “For how long?”

“Another day, and then we must go.” She held up a striped skirt to her waist. “I willnae need to feed for another threeday.”

Gavin wondered if that’d been for her benefit or his. Perhaps Thora did care for him, if in her own way. He went to the front room’s hearth and built a fire. Eventually Thora emerged dressed as a farmer’s wife.

“You look lovely,” he said.

“I think not but…” She nodded at the spot where the coffin had been. “You took them out?”

“I buried them,” Gavin admitted. “It was the decent thing to do.”

“Yes,” she said quietly, regarding him. “’Twas.”

She sat down in one of the blanket-covered chairs by the fire, and stared into the flames. "When the Pritani attacked my village, my brother distracted them long enough for me to reach my father's boat. I sailed away from the island to Orkney, and from there to Norrvegr. I had no tribe left, so I was obliged to work as a serving maid to a jarl." She met his gaze. "He had lost his only sons to the Pritani, and took pity on me. When I asked him if I could train as a shield-maiden, he sent me to the finest war camp to be taught the ways of battle. I fought every day to grow stronger and faster, until I was prepared."

Gavin sat down in the chair beside hers as they talked long into the night. He listened as she spoke of her life among the Viking warriors. It hadn't taken her long to rise through the ranks and be given her own long boat. Her first raid had been on a Pritani ship, which she had captured and brought back as plunder for her jarl.

"My men took a share, but all I wanted were the survivors," Thora said, her eyes going dreamy. "I put them to the stake, and burned them alive, so they could know what my tribe suffered. 'Twas not decent, but for the first time I felt I could hold up my head and call myself Viking."

"But one ship wasn't enough," Gavin guessed.

She tossed a chunk of pine onto the fire, making it flare. "I vowed that I wouldnae rest until I put to the flame every Pritani that drew breath. I very nearly did before I died in battle." She glanced at him. "You carry yourself like a warrior. The lion and the cross on your shoulder, are they symbols of your tribe?"

He'd never thought of The Black Watch as a tribe, but it certainly fit. "Yes, but we didn't fight here in Scotland. My regiment was sent overseas to the Middle East to fight terrorists."

"Battles change, but warriors never do." Her eyes shifted to the window as she quickly straightened. She cocked her head as she listened. "Someone approaches."

Gavin went to the window, and looked both ways. "I don't see anyone."

When he glanced over his shoulder he saw that Thora had gone back into the bed chamber, where he found her stripping off the dead woman's clothing.

She gestured at her modified Roman legion uniform. "I must wear that. Bring it to me."

Gavin helped her quickly dress, then tucked his dirk in his belt as he followed her out into the night. Thora strode into the south pasture and crossed the field, peering ahead until the sound of horses moving toward them made her halt.

The undead Romans looked as astonished to see her as Gavin felt to see them. The men muttered in Latin to each other as they trotted forward to peer at Thora.

"Patrol, halt," Thora barked out. "Did you bring the horses for us?"

She sounded so much like Fenella that Gavin flinched.

"Hail, Prefect Ivar," said the man leading the patrol. He dismounted, dropped on his knee and struck his chestplate with his fisted hand in a salute. "We were not told that you were in this area. Highlanders have been spotted, and we were sent to scout them."

Thora nodded. "I cannae wait any longer

for resupply. You will give me two of your mounts, now. When is the next transport ship to arrive here?"

"Sunset this night." The Roman stood and motioned to two of the men, who dismounted and brought their horses to Gavin. "You dinnae sound much like yourself, Prefect." He glanced around. "And where are the rest of your men?"

Thora sighed and spoke to Gavin. "The prefect was much hated and I am merciless. I'm afraid 'tis a lethal combination, for I cannae stop until I have Freyja's Eye and my vengeance. Mayhaps you should turn away."

She plucked the dirk from Gavin's belt, and disappeared in a blur.

Bile rose in his throat as he watched her flash through the patrol, slicing and stabbing as the Romans disintegrated into ash. Though the last man tried to flee, she was on him in a second. Then she saw that Gavin was watching.

"Pick up the weapons they dropped," she told him.

But rather than finish the soldier, her hand flew to her face. As a shaft of sunlight struck her, she let out a screech of pain. The sun had crested the horizon without any of them seeing it through the dense forest.

As Gavin tossed Thora over his shoulder, he saw the scorched Roman crawling away into the brush. He ran for the house, kicking in the door and rushing into the bed chamber.

"I didnae finish him," Thora protested as he put her on her feet. She grabbed the front of his tunic. "I must do it."

He looked at her hands, which were covered with ash. One still grasped the dagger. "The sun has already burnt him," he said hotly and touched the singe mark on her face. "As it might have you, Thora. Your body is undead. You cannae behave as you did when you were mortal." Though her reddish-brown eyes blazed back at him, he watched as she tamped down her fury. "Give me the blade."

Though she hesitated, she passed it to him handle first. He slashed his palm. As the blood trickled down his fingers, he brushed them over her face, healing the burn. Then he took her hands in his. To have them burned so must have been excruciating. As he healed them he began to see her in a new light.

Wiping out the Pritani would never bring back her tribe. He doubted it would even give her peace. But that she had to see this through, no matter the cost, was now obvious —as was the fact that she couldn't do it on her own.

"We will leave at sundown," he said.

## Chapter Eighteen

SHARING HER HUSBAND'S immortal soul also came with a few extra benefits for Diana, but the one she liked most was water-traveling. It saved so much time when they had to cross long distances. When she came out of the river, she changed back into her physical form.

"Especially convenient when hunting renegade Vikings," she said to herself, "finding invisible future chicks and their enthralled brothers, and, of course, the undead who've been possessed by the renegade Vikings' sister." She found Raen and Evander staring at her. "What? None of this is my fault. I let them escape so they could rescue the brother."

"'Twas a kindness," her husband said and

looked at the captain. "Dinnae you agree, Talorc?"

"Oh, aye. Just as when I escaped with Fiona, and speared you through the throat when you tried to stop us." His mouth twitched before he bent to check the bundle of spears he'd brought. "I did it for love."

"No' for love of me," Raen muttered.

"I liked you two better when you hated each other," Diana said and studied the surrounding terrain for any trace of Tormod's trail. "Oh, great."

Hundreds of mortal trails crisscrossed the ground and overlapped each other, probably the tracks of locals coming back and forth to the river for water. On the plus side, she saw no sign of the undead or any of their enthralled minions in the trails.

"I think we need to get away from the– Oh, wait."

Leading up from the bank was a faint, broken trail of bright blue that she recognized as Tormod's track. When she knelt down to study it she saw the breaks in the trail were overlaps of a colorless track, which had to belong to Jema.

She ros

them. This

his throat sh

ized both me

sorry." Mu

summoned a

clothes.

Tormod's

where it haltec ...vander went inside to make inquiries, and returned to confirm that the Viking had taken a room.

"He came alone, and told the innkeeper no' to disturb him for the day." The captain glanced up at the windows overhead. "I reckon Jema cloaked herself so her garments wouldnae be questioned."

"They're probably sleeping, or doing what we all do before we conk out." Diana dragged her teeth over her bottom lip as she considered their options. The sun would be setting in less than six hours, but until it did Thora would not be able to emerge from wherever she was hiding with Gavin until nightfall. "Let me go in alone."

Diana sent Evander and Raen to distract the innkeeper while she went upstairs. With





every step she took she

shoulders increase

she'd tell the Vi

"Your

vampir

"G

…felt the weight on her … She still wasn't sure what …king.

…sister reincarnated, only she's a … now," she muttered under her breath. …ood news, you don't have to keep looking for her grave. Bad news, she needs to be put back into one." She stopped at the threshold of the room and thought of the one thing she could actually say to him with real honesty. "Come home. Just please come home."

Diana jumped as the door swung open, and a bare-chested, tousle-haired Tormod peered out at her.

"Red," he said and stepped out into the hall and closed the door. "You tracked us?"

In that moment Diana saw him not as he was, but as the boy he had been. He would have been tall and gawky as a teenager, she thought, and no match for Lachlan and his Pritani warriors. She could see him taunting them, and running around the burning homes of his tribe as he tried to buy his sister enough time to get to the boat. He'd risked his life for her. He'd sacrificed his freedom.

No way would he do anything to hurt Thora. Then or now.

Diana had never hated herself so much as she did in this moment. "The laird sent me to find you," she said quickly. "Raen and Evander came, too. We'll help you get Jema's brother back."

The Viking grinned. "Am I forgiven?"

Diana couldn't muster a smile in return. "You'll probably be scrubbing out privies for the next hundred years, but yeah." She nodded past him. "Scotty okay?"

"Aye. She's bonny and brilliant and all a man could hope to have." Dreams filled his eyes. "As soon as we end Fenella and save Gavin, we'll be marrying. Can you fathom it? Me, a husband."

She wanted to hug him but her lie of omission was suddenly like a wall between them. "Congratulations," she said, looking away. "I'm going to take the guys and do some scouting around town. We'll be back before dark."

Diana headed back downstairs, but took the steps slower this time. Instead of the crushing weight of shame, she felt numb. It didn't help when she found the men bickering in low voices.

"Telling the Viking that 'tis his sister who possesses Fenella's body is madness," Raen insisted. "She has already tried to kill the laird. She wasnae known as Thora the Merciless for naught. She will use Tormod and his resentment of the clan to take her revenge, and likely kill both of the McShanes in the doing."

"Tormod is wiser than you ken," Evander countered. "Once he learns Thora means to use this cursed jewel to slaughter the entire clan, he will stand with us."

Diana wanted to agree with the captain. She knew the Viking didn't share his sister's desire for vengeance. What gave her pause was the last of what he'd said: *he will stand with us.*

"I couldn't tell him," Diana said tightly as she passed them and left the inn. She kept going until she stood on the rocky edge of the shore, where she watched the waves until her husband joined her and put his arm around her shoulders. She leaned against him, taking a little comfort from the warmth and strength he radiated. "Will Evander give him the news?"

"No' for now. Once Lachlan and the warband arrive, we'll reconsider." His mouth hitched as she stared at him. "When the clan is threatened, the laird doesnae cower and hide at home. He gave us an hour so you might decide what the Viking should ken."

"Why me?" she said, her eyes stinging with the start of tears. She put up a hand to stop his answer, already knowing what it was. "Because I'm the cop."

"No, my lady," Raen said and stroked her damp cheek. "Because you are the sister of Tormod's heart."

Tormod searched through the crumpled linens on the empty bed, and then glanced under the ticking. "Diana has left, Jema. You dinnae need cloak yourself any longer." When she didn't respond his search became more frantic. "Where are you, my lass? Speak to me, now, before I tear apart the room."

The door creaked open and shut, and

Jema materialized, naked but for his tunic. In her hands she held two mugs of hot brew.

"Wench, oft times you terrify me." He started toward her, his pace slowing to a stop as he saw her strained expression. "You've seen the others. They've no' come to capture us. The laird sent them to help us take back Gavin."

She nodded, and set the mugs aside before she went to close the window shutters. "I have to tell you something." At last she came to him, and took his hands in hers.

She looked so miserable he didn't try to jest. "This cannae be good. Mayhap you should no'."

"I don't want to," Jema admitted. "But if it were Gavin, I would want to know."

What Jema told him next fell on his ears like the blows of heavy fists. She repeated everything she'd overheard Raen, Evander and Diana say while she'd stood just a few feet away. Because she had been cloaked downstairs they hadn't realized she was listening.

When she finished he couldn't move. "Surely no' this. No' come back as undead. The gods wouldnae be so cruel."

"Gavin is with her," she said softly. "He's a good man. He'll protect her."

The paralyzing shock released him, and he backed away from her. "He'll have no choice. She enslaved him." He peered at her. "Why would Red keep this from me?"

Jema hugged her waist with her arms. "Maybe she thought it would put you in an impossible situation."

"Aye. 'Tis that." Tormod sat down on the bed and propped his head in his hands as he tried to fathom it. "Fenella must have found the crypt. 'Twas likely close to the portal where you crossed over with Gavin." He shoved his raging emotions deep inside and locked them away before he looked up at his lady. "I must find Thora before the clan does."

"I know," Jema said and came to him. When he pulled her onto his lap she pressed her cheek to his shoulder. "There's a back way out through the kitchen. We'll leave the inn before they return."

He drew back to regard her. "Such a canny lass. You've already found a way out?"

She smiled and nodded. "We should try to

rouse my Viking spirit and see if she can help us."

Her words cut through him like a hail of scythes. Jema spoke of arousing the Aesir as if the spirit that possessed her was simply an ally waiting to provide wisdom and guidance. He'd never told her of the nature of the Viking gods. They demanded respect and reverence from all mortals while showing very little regard for their lives. If given enough control, the spirit would use her. If that happened, her fate would be little different than that of Fenella Ivar. And that, he could never allow.

"Is there another way?" she asked, as if she could hear what he was thinking. "Maybe you should tell Diana that you know about Thora. She helped us escape Dun Aran. I know she would try to help with your sister."

Tormod steeled himself for what had to happen next. Gently, he held Jema's lovely face between his big hands and tipped up her chin to look into his eyes. "Give me a kiss for luck."

Jema sighed against his lips, opening for him, and shivered as he drew her down to lay beneath him. But as his lips enveloped hers, he smoothly shifted his fingers down. He pressed gently but firmly against the two pulsing veins in her throat. For a moment her eyelids fluttered and she tried to say something, but he kept kissing her until her body went limp a few moments later. Tormod took his hands from her neck and checked her breathing and heartbeat before he stood.

"You will be safe here. Diana and the men will return to set you free. Gods willing, I shall return to you for a sound scolding. You may even beat me if you wish."

Though it grated fiercely on him to do it, he ripped the bed linens into strips and used them to tie her to the bed. He bent down to kiss her one last time.

"I love you, lass."

Jema's lips parted, and a melodic, unearthly voice came out of her mouth. "The chaos will not end with ice, son of Arn. Fire must also play her part."

He backed away from the bed as the rage boiled up inside him. "I give myself to the Aesir, but you cannae have her. If my life is no' enough then fack you and Odin and Asgard to Hel."

The golden arrow from Jema's arm shot through the air, stopping to hover an inch from Tormod's right eye.

*I, too, loved,* the voice whispered inside his head. *Thora the Merciless offered her heart and vowed her devotion. Yet when I gave her my most powerful and precious jewel, she used it to betray me. When she would not return it, I cursed her.*

Tormod scowled. Thora cursed? She'd been the chosen of the Aesir from the day of her birth. But then he thought back on her burial. It had evaded him for centuries in its remote location and hidden with cunning traps. There was naught about it that spoke of honoring her life as a shieldmaiden. No, it had been secreted away as one would bury the plague.

"I am not Thora," he said, holding out his arms. "Use me. I shall be your vessel. There is no one she trusts more than her brother."

*So be it.* The arrow darted down, piercing his sleeve and burying itself in his skinwork. *I will guide you to her, son of Arn. Together we will take back what she has stolen.*

Tormod pulled back his tunic, gritting his teeth as the golden arrow etched itself in the center of his skinwork. The design of his helm rippled and changed, becoming a circle of map points with the arrow pointing north.

Looking at Jema, he felt a little better. She would be safe, and all the risk of carrying the Aesir would be his. In time, he hoped she would forgive him.

He picked up the axe, and tucked it in his belt. To the arrow he said, “Take me to Thora, Freyja.”

## Chapter Nineteen

THE MOMENT THE sun set Quintus opened his eyes, and stared up at the moldy wood of the deck overhead. He had never favored traveling by boat. The stink of the ocean permeated everything. Having an island stronghold required the use of the black ships, but the McDonnels had before proven they could send them to the bottom of the sea. He would not be at ease again until he recovered Fenella and returned to the safety of Staffa.

An hour later a knock came at the door to his cabin, and the mortal captain of the ship entered. “Forgive the intrusion, Tribune. This message came with the supply boat from Tarvodobran. The centurion on deck said you would wish to see it at once." The captain bowed before he offered a scroll.

Since Fenella had vanished Quintus had felt an inexplicable and growing sense of urgency. From the evidence found at the forest grave site her men had all died to protect her. He'd ordered all the mainland patrols to search for her while he'd hunted through his library for more stories about Freyja's Eye. References to the disastrous sea battle repeatedly warned against sailing near a small island near the waters where all the ships had sunk. In every text the same reason had been cited: the island had been cursed by the gods. Since the Ninth Legion had been made undead under very similar circumstances Quintus wondered if the Eye might provide more than leverage against the McDonnel Clan.

From the scroll, Quintus read the alarming news that an entire patrol had been wiped out at a farm in the highlands. One centurion had survived by crawling into the farmer's grain storage fougou, where he was able to heal and wait for darkness. The sole survivor claimed that Fenella Ivar alone was responsible for slaughtering his patrol, and would likely try to steal a black ship.

Quintus consulted his map of the coast and the roster of the ships' schedules. The only ship in the region was the supply boat, the *Ebon*.

"Extinguish all the lights. Have the look-outs watch for the *Ebon*."

"At once, Tribune," the mortal said and hesitated. "Your chamber wench awaits your command."

"Send her in." Quintus rolled up the map and stowed it in his trunk.

The female mortal who came into the room had dressed in a fine gown, and wore her dull brown hair in a single long braid. Like all blood thralls she appeared happy and eager to please him. She dropped into a deep curtsey before she reached for the fasteners on her bodice.

"No," Quintus ordered and stared at her as he remembered the placid blue of Fenella's eyes when she had been mortal. "What is your name?"

"Bryn, milord." She bobbed a second time. Sturdy and plump, she had rounded cheeks that made her eyes almost disappear when she smiled. “How may I please you?”

As his mortal thrall Fenella had been as eager, and he had fallen in love with her. It had been that love that had compelled him to turn her after Ermindale had tried to kill her. Fenella had been a dangerous distraction, his former prefect had claimed, and later he predicted she would turn on Quintus. Knowing the marquess had been right in his suspicions was a bitter draught to swallow.

“Milord?” Bryn said sounding hopeful, even when she had no hope.

He focused on the mortal, and for the first time saw the paleness of her flesh. She might survive another feeding or two, but no more. She would die of blood loss, gasping for breath as Fenella had. But if Quintus turned Bryn, would she become as vicious? Or could he mold this female into something more than a selfish, greedy killer like Fenella? Though she’d had her faults, she’d been quite useful.

“What were you before you came to us?” he asked as he tugged up Bryn’s sleeve.

“A hoor in the town of Pennan, milord.”

She sidled closer to him as she offered him her wrist. "Shall I lift my skirts?"

"No, my dear," Quintus said and bit into her flesh, drinking her hot blood until her knees gave way. He bore her to the deck, draping her over his arm and draining her until he felt her heartbeat stutter. Then he tore a gash in his own wrist, and pressed her mouth to it. Feeling her drink his tainted blood filled him with an unexpected, savage satisfaction.

For reasons still mysterious to Quintus, turning a female mortal to undead took less time than with a male. The process also proved much more violent, so once she had taken enough of his blood he carried her over to his bed and shackled her to it.

Bryn smiled up at him. "Thank you, milord."

"Rest now, my dear." As she died and began her conversion, he covered her face with the blanket. "When you awake, we shall have much to do."

Quintus went to the upper deck and joined two of his centurions at the front of the ship. Running without lights made them virtually invisible to the shore as well as other vessels, and his men had taken positions at the railings to keep watch for the *Ebon*.

"Advise your men that Fenella Ivar no longer serves the Ninth as prefect," he told one of the centurions as he watched the waters. "She is to be treated as a traitor, but take care. I do not want her killed until we recover the Eye. Once we have the jewel, you will bring her to me in shackles."

Until she was a prisoner, Quintus had no intention of being near her.

The captain hurried over to them and pointed to a cluster of lights moving north. "A black ship departs the docks at Tarvodobran, my lord."

Quintus felt calm finally settle over him. "Change course and follow it."

❧

JERKING on the bindings that Tormod had left her in proved useless. Unless Jema got help she'd be stuck on the bed until Diana found her or her lover came back.

She felt completely ridiculous. She'd been

so busy kissing her Viking that she hadn't even felt the pressure he'd used on her throat until a few seconds before she blacked out. She should be furious with him, but when she saw the golden arrow missing from her forearm she understood. He'd offered himself to the Aesir again, sacrificing himself to save her.

Jema couldn't let that happen.

"Help!" she called out. "Help!"

Though it took a few more yells, the door to the room finally rattled and then swung open. A maid stopped in her tracks, her jaw dropping as she saw Jema.

"Please, help me," she said, and hated herself as she added, "I've been stolen from my family by that Viking."

"Oh, ye poor thing," the girl said and rushed over and untied the strips of bedding. Once she helped Jema to her feet, she said, "I'll summon the sheriff's men. They'll find the bastart."

"He went south to steal horses," Jema told her, and waited for her to leave before changing into her clothes and cloaking herself.

Rushing out of the inn through the kitchen door, Jema tried to think where Tormod would go. But seeing that it was night made her fear spike. He could already be gone.

A familiar burning on her chest made her duck between two buildings to uncloak. When she pulled out the map disc, its fine etchings already glowed with white light. Though she had no map to shine it on, she pointed it at the ground. A series of circles and triangles illuminated in sequence one after another, and as she followed the direction of their travel, they pointed directly to the town's main pier.

"Please be right," Jema murmured as she cloaked herself and ran for the docks.

A number of boats and small fishing vessels had been tied to the pier posts, and Jema had to weave her way through a busy cluster of men unloading the day's catch from nets into a huge cart. Once she got past them she saw several empty dories and one last boat where a man was raising a sail.

*Tormod.*

Moving as silently as she could, Jema walked down the last stretch of planks until she stood beside the sail boat. Tormod tied off the sail and reached for the rope around the pier post, when he suddenly looked up into her eyes.

"Fack me," he muttered, but then shook his head and shoulders as if throwing off a chill.

Jema barely had time to step onto the side deck as he cast off. Her Viking steered the boom so that the sail caught the wind. The narrow hull began to cut through the water as the boat moved away from the docks.

With hardly any empty space on the upper deck, Jema was forced to stand against the main mast. Tormod was only a few feet away, close enough that if he stretched out an arm he could touch her. She started to sigh and then caught herself. If she made any noise he would find her, and turn the boat around to take her back to the inn.

His shoulder suddenly glowed with light, and while Tormod looked down at it he adjusted his course.

So the Aesir were guiding him, she thought. No wonder he hadn't used his water-travel. He needed to see the tattoo.

Anger flooded Jema as she stared at the golden arrow. The Gods, if there really were any, expected too much from Tormod. Hadn't he suffered enough? When would they finally be done with him?

Jema bit her lip as her forearm grew hot, and something on her cheek did the same.

*It is time for you to hide again, blood of Anea, blood of Eryk*, a melodic voice said inside Jema's thoughts. *Tormod will find his sister, but you must find the jewel. You will bring it to him, or your lover will die.*

*How can I find the Eye when I don't know where it is?* She winced as her arm seemed to catch fire. *Yes, right. You're all powerful. You're going to show me.*

*I will show him where to find his sister. He will keep her distracted while you do your work.* The spirit's voice grew flinty. *Do not disappoint us, Jema McShane. He is long beloved of the Aesir. We will see the son of Arn rewarded for his valiance.*

Jema looked at the lantern light gilding her Viking's face. *So will I.*

---

THE SIGHT of the black ship anchored just beyond the skerry made Tormod extinguish his lantern. Once he drew close enough, he took down the sail and dove over the side of the boat. Swimming through the icy sea water, he thought of Jema, and wished now he hadn't left her at the inn. He could have taken her to Diana, or explained why she couldn't go with him. He might have asked her to wait for him, but it was too late now.

Tormod used the rocky outcroppings on the shore as cover, and moved carefully inland. The tiny island appeared to be mostly rock that was honeycombed with tidal tunnels. It was topped by a mound of shell and driftwood built up around a narrow depression in the ground. Waves crashed all around the skerry, misting the air with spindrift. As Tormod scaled the rocks, he looked out for nests before he took a handhold. That was when he realized there were no birds anywhere, nor crabs or voles or even hares.

Could it be that not a single living creature resided on the island?

A flickering torch appeared on the opposite side of the mound, carried by a big man dressed in a hunter's tunic and jacket, with faded blue trews like Jema's. He looked pale but determined, and from the muscle that strained at the tunic's seams he'd be a brute in a fight.

*Gavin.* Tormod crouched down to watch as Jema's brother stopped to look around the mound before glancing over his shoulder and nodding. While he was looking away Tormod changed positions, gaining enough elevation to see inside the pit. Dark, churning water filled a perfect oval in the center of the mound.

A sea well, fed by the island's tidal tunnels had been cut off from the ocean.

Tormod flinched as Fenella Ivar walked into the torchlight, her golden hair now a rich dark brown, and her eyes no longer black. She had dressed herself like a farmer, and for a moment he wondered if it were all a terrible ruse. Then Fenella bent down to pick up a shell, and with a flip of her wrist tossed it into the sea well.

Closing his eyes could not remove the memory of Thora doing the same thing on the shores of Skye as she threw rocks into the sea. The heat in his shoulder vanished as he stood, drawing the axe from his belt. He stepped into the light cast by Gavin's torch.

"You cannae tell how deep it goes with a shell. You must drop a stone tied to a rope, and mark the top when it reaches bottom."

Before he finished speaking Gavin had shoved the torch into Thora's hands and stepped in front of her as he brandished a dirk. "You're not wanted. Get out of here."

Saying the words that he never imagined he would again made him smile. "Fair evening, Thora."

Tormod's sister touched Gavin's arm, pushing at it until he lowered the blade. She tilted her head as she walked to the very edge of the sea well.

"No," she whispered as she studied him like she might a leprous brigand. "You cannae trick me. My brother died saving me from the Pritani. You arenae Tormod."

"That day I told you to go, and no' to look back at me," he said gently. "You were a good lass and did exactly that as you ran away. I saw you reach the cove, and then I went in the other direction to lead them off. They didn't kill me, Sister. They–"

"No," Thora shrieked. "Tormod lives with the gods. They rewarded him for his sacrifice. Freyja promised they would. She swore it."

"Mayhap they will someday." He started walking around the well toward her. "Thora, I was made a slave by the Pritani. I served them for ten years before the Romans came and I was freed." He glanced down. "I never thought I would miss you putting frogs in my boots, but I did."

She gasped and covered her mouth with a trembling hand. But in the next instant she blurred around the edge of the sea well and flung herself at him. He caught her and hugged her so fiercely that he thought they might crush each other. All the centuries of searching and being alone had ended. As Thora sobbed against his chest, his throat tightened lest he do the same.

For his part Gavin merely stood and watched them both, his expression guarded.

*He isnae enthralled,* Tormod thought as Thora finally quieted.

"I cannae cry in this body," she whispered. "Undead cannae make tears. If I could, Brother, I would fill an ocean with them."

"We neednae weep," he said quietly and

felt the last crack in his heart mend. "'Tis a happiness that we are together again, Sister."

"Did the gods send you back to me?" She stepped back to look up at him. "Was it Freyja? Has she forgiven me?"

Tormod shook his head. "Why did you offer yourself to the goddess?"

"I ken if I won her favor that she would bestow wonders on me," Thora said, smiling a little. "She plucked the eye from her face and made it a love gift. She bade me to wear it, like a bauble, but I knew what to do with it." She shrugged. "It sank all of the Pritani ships that tried to stop us." She inspected him. "You are no' like the Romans, I can see that. How are you come here to me?"

The time for the reckoning had arrived.

"I was made immortal, Thora," Tormod told her. "'Twas my reward for protecting the magic folk from the Romans. For that I was killed, and then brought back to live forever. So were the Pritani who fought with me."

The pleasure went out of Thora's face, snuffed out as quickly as a pinched candle. "*What* did you say?"

# Chapter Twenty

"MY MASTERS DIDNAE abuse me as a slave," Tormod said. "In time I began to look upon them more as brothers."

"No. I dinnae believe you." She stepped back from him.

"Then came the Romans, like a plague spreading across Caledonia. They hunted the druids, who couldnae defend themselves." He told her of their last stand on Skye, and how they had been slaughtered and thrown into the loch. "When the magic folk learned of our sacrifice, they cast our deaths onto the Romans. The clan awoke as immortals who need never again die."

"The clan," she ground out past a

clenched jaw. Her eyes glittered as she bared her teeth. "You joined the Pritani's tribe. The Pritani who put to the flame our people, our village, our parents. The Pritani who stole everything I loved from me. How could you kiss the arses of those murderers?"

Now she sounded like the petulant little girl who had thrown tantrums whenever anyone denied her wants. "'Twas us who first burned their village while they were away burying their chieftain. They faced the starvation and cold of the winter. Of course they were angry. Had they done so to us, striking first, would we no' have retaliated?"

"You talk like a traitor," she said and spat at his feet.

"Think what you will of me," Tormod said. "The clan and I protect mortal kind now. I ken why you came here, Thora. You cannae use Freyja's Eye again. You know what will happen if you do."

"Give me your blade, Gavin," she said, holding out her hand. When the big man came to her he placed it on her palm. She took it and jerked him down to his knees. Seizing a handful of his dark hair, Thora hauled Gavin's head back and put the dirk to his throat.

Jema's brother looked thunderstruck. "Thora?"

"Shut up," she said to him before addressing Tormod, who drew his axe. "You are no brother of mine, Tormod Liefson. Nor shall you stop me from seeking justice for our tribe. You say you protect mortal kind now?" She pressed in the blade enough to make Gavin bleed. "Go from this place now, or I will slit his throat and bathe in his blood."

❧

Jema's chest stopped burning as soon as she reached the sea well. There she crouched, unseen by anyone, and stared at her brother.

*Oh my god, Gee.*

Gavin's wasted body had vanished, replaced by the heavy, muscular frame he'd had during his military days. Seeing him so vital and alive made Jema take in a shuddering breath as tears sprang into her eyes. Though Tormod had said he would be healed, it was nothing short of a miracle.

But when Thora pressed the blade to Gavin's throat, Jema had to clamp a hand over her own mouth to keep from screaming. She watched Tormod drop his axe, and saw the bleak worry in his expression as he tried persuading Thora to release her brother.

*It is time now, beloved of Tormod,* the spirit said inside her mind. *Look down into the well. There you shall see the Eye.*

Jema blinked away her tears and leaned over to spot a tiny sparkle in the depths of the well. *That has to be a hundred feet down.*

*Yes.*

She wanted to scream with frustration. *I have no equipment, and I'm not an expert swimmer. Do you want me to drown?*

*We want you to defy chaos and create that which will be forever.* The voice grew chilly. *Bring the Eye to Tormod and your men shall be saved.*

That was the only reason she had come. She looked down into the water again. It was deep but it had to be done. She moved to the edge.

Diving in would create a splash that would give away her presence. Instead Jema swung her legs over the side of the well, and slipped into the freezing water. When it closed over her head she swam for the bottom as fast as she could.

Light from the torch filtered down and met the sparkling glow that began to rise up around her. Tiny coral and shellfish lined the sides of the well, providing homes for even tinier fish. The lower she went, the more the inhabitants seem to pick up the tangerine light from beneath, until it looked as if the sides of the well were on fire.

*Freyja's Eye.*

Jema felt the pressure in her ears, head and chest growing painful. The soul-numbing temperature of the water also felt as if it were seeping into her bones. Finally she was able to touch the silty bottom. From that soft layer she uncovered a fist-sized jewel carved to look like a drowsy eye. The moment she touched it the diamond opened and stared at her like a living thing. Yet when she tried to take it from the well bottom it wouldn't budge.

*No, no.* Sweeping away more of the silt, she saw that the diamond lay partially embedded in what appeared to be melted rock. *I can't excavate it. I have no tools, and I'm running out of time.*

*You were brought back for this, Jema McShane. Use your knowledge and skills.*

Her lungs ached, and the need to breathe was becoming overwhelming. Jema searched around the Eye frantically until she found a large rock. Helped by the buoyancy of the water, she lifted it with both hands. With all her might, she swung it at the melted rock. A dull thunk resounded in her ears. Over and over she brought her hammerstone down, ringing the diamond with pits and cracks in its surrounding matrix.

But the pain in her lungs was excruciating. Another second and she'd have to ascend for air. But as she dropped her makeshift tool, she saw the stone and diamond separate from the floor. She snatched it in one hand, turned, and made for the surface.

*Please, just let me last a little longer.*

She was coming up too fast and not stopping to allow her body to adjust to the change in pressure. If she didn't pass out and drown, an air embolism would cause her to stroke out or have a heart attack.

*All of this wouldn't have happened if I was simply going to die and sink to the bottom with this damned rock.* Jema had never prayed in anger, but now seemed the time to start. *Goddess, this was your mission. Damn it, help me finish it.*

A single shaft of blazing gold light shot upward from the diamond. But quickly it refracted into hundreds of others. The beams turned the well into a cauldron of seething molten power. A tremendous force smashed into Jema, driving her upward but also to the side. As her head and back collided with the wall of the well, the last of her air burst from her mouth. Reflexively she inhaled and filled her chest with sea water.

She wrapped her hands around the Eye as she began to sink. Warmth was spreading from the back of her head and the water was clouding with red. She had no strength to swim or kick or even keep her eyes open, but she would keep the diamond safe.

That had to count for something.

Dimly she heard a muffled sound like a heavy splash, and then silence filled her ears. She felt the effervescence of the water being displaced in front of her, and her skin turned to ice. She managed to open her eyes to slits and saw her Viking holding her as he swam back up to the surface. But just as they came out into the air she went blind. With the last of her strength, she pushed the diamond into his grip, her hands covering his as all her senses failed.

She tasted the salt of tears on her lips. His, hers, or was it just the sea? Did it matter?

How lovely it had been, finding this man, and learning to love him. Her heart, which gave its last slow beat, filled with joy. He would live, and so would her brother, and her part in that was done.

---

DIANA PACED BACK and forth on the deck of the fisher they had taken from the dock. "How can you people have not invented the outboard motor?"

"Lights out," the laird called, and the clan extinguished the deck lanterns.

The silhouette of two black ships showed against the night sky, each far enough away from the skerry to prevent running aground.

On the island itself a flickering torch provided the only light, which showed two, no, three figures standing on top of a mound.

Raen caught Diana's arm as she rushed toward the side.

"What are we waiting for?" she demanded.

Evander pointed to the side of one of the black ships, where dozens of Romans were dropping into the sea.

"They won't see us in our water-traveling forms," she told him.

"Not us," Raen told her. "You must stay here."

"They'll use Jema to work him," she said. "He loves her. If I don't talk to him, he'll give Thora the Eye to save her."

"No, he willnae," Lachlan said, joining them. "Tormod can be just as merciless as his sister."

"He'll listen to me," Diana insisted.

"Diana," Evander said. "I ken that you wish to save the Viking. But 'tis no' your fight now. We must trust that he 'twill do what is necessary, the same as us."

Lachlan eyed the skerry and nodded to Evander. "'Tis time."

"You've no gun," Raen told her as the other members of the warband began slipping over the side. "And there's no place to run if you attract the undead with your blood." He took her by the arms. "I'll see to your Viking, but I must ken that you are safe."

Reluctantly Diana nodded and placed a hand over his heart. "Just make sure you come back."

---

TORMOD HELD Jema as he climbed out of the well, the huge golden diamond caught between their bodies. He carried her to the nearest level spot, and gently lowered her to the ground. He could feel the terrible injury to the back of her head. But looking at her pale, peaceful face he knew that she had drowned. His trembling hand caressed her cheek as a deep, numbing shock settled in his bones.

"My sweet lass," he whispered, as his voice strained and then broke. Gently he moved a lock of hair from her cold forehead. "What have you done?"

Water from his own damp hair dripped into her face, which he could hardly see now from the water in his eyes.

"The Eye," Thora called to him from the other side of the sea well. "Did she find it?"

"Jema?" Gavin said. "*Jema?*" Tormod finally raised his gaze to look at Jema's brother across the well. Gavin's face was frozen in a paroxysm of horror. "*No*."

But before Tormod could reply, the sound of hobnail boots made both Thora and Gavin turn about. Dozens of undead were walking out of the sea onto the rocky shore. Tormod seized the diamond and grabbed his axe. But there weren't dozens of undead, there were hundreds.

A centurion walked to the front of his men and looked at Thora with unconcealed hatred. "Fenella Ivar, you no longer serve the Ninth Legion. You have been implicated in the murder of your fellow soldiers by a survivor of your attack. You have disgraced your position and betrayed the trust placed in you by

Tribune Quintus Seneca. Surrender yourself to us now or die here."

"There are too many," Gavin said to her and put a hand on her arm. "Even with your speed. We must run."

She yanked her arm away from him, still facing the centurion. "Thora the Merciless doesnae run."

The centurion raised his sword and pointed at her but when he opened his mouth to give an order, he quickly shut it. All of the Romans backed up a pace.

Thora threw her head back and barked a short laugh. "Do you see what cowards they are?" she said, her voice dripping with disgust.

But Gavin wasn't listening to her. Instead he turned to look past Tormod, who then followed his gaze.

Though Tormod had to keep his jaw from falling open, his chest threatened to burst with pride. His clan had arrived.

As Lachlan approached, he gazed down at the still form of Jema and his mouth twisted in a cruel grimace. As he passed, his eyes met Tormod's and the laird gave him a stiff nod, which Tormod returned.

Next was Raen. "Did you find it?"

In response, Tormod finally held up the diamond. To say it was beautiful was to insult the gem. It was like sunlight itself captured in purest crystal. The hands that had carved it to resemble an eye had belonged to a master of the craft. Not a single imperfection marred the glittering jewel. Nothing he had seen or would ever see, he suspected, would ever match its stunning flawlessness.

"Good lad," the big man said. "Keep it safe while we separate these worthless beasts from their fanged heads."

As Lachlan rounded the well, he broke into a trot and drew both his swords. "Clan McDonnel," he bellowed. "Heid doon, arse up!"

Raen, Evander, and the rest of the warband followed. They waded into the enemy in a clashing, slashing maelstrom of flying steel. But as the ash of the undead began to litter the soil, one person stood apart. Tormod watched as Thora's hungry eyes fixed on the gem in his hand. In a blur she was around the sea well and wrenching Freyja's Eye from his grasp.

But Tormod was not going to give up so easily. His Jema had died for the damn thing's sake. He locked his large hands on it as she tugged with all her might.

"No, Thora," he said through clenched teeth. Her undead body was strong. "Leave it be."

"You fool," she shrieked. "It is the instrument of our victory."

"'Tis a weapon of the Aesir and no' to be trusted. They let Jema die for it, and who knows their reasons."

"Coward," she grunted, tugging so hard that she spun him around her. "I ken its power." Her eyes locked on his. "I sent my own fleet to the bottom with it."

"What?" he said, almost losing his grip.

"I slaughtered them all!" she screamed. "Viking and Pritani alike. I'd have killed as many of our own people as needed to see every Pritani die."

Tormod couldn't believe it but then he remembered the words of Freyja.

*Yet when I gave her my most powerful and precious jewel, she used it to betray me.*

"Aye," Thora confirmed. "'Twas I who

destroyed both sides. The same as I'll do now."

As she uttered the last, she flung her head forward, smashing the top of it into his face. Though he reeled from the blow, Tormod didn't let go. Not until she pushed off of him with a savage kick to his stomach did his fingers finally come loose. They flew apart, both landing on their backs.

Tormod rolled to keep from being trampled. The fighting had come close. Though the clan battled ferociously, the steady press of Roman bodies was forcing them back. Even Gavin had picked up a sword and was killing the undead as fast as they came at him.

Thora scrambled to her feet and thrust the jewel above her head. "Freyja, your daughter calls on you!"

Frantically Tormod looked about him for a weapon. His axe lay on the ground where he'd dropped it next to Jema. As warriors clashed around him, he stooped and snatched it up. But as he rose, a flurry of ash flew into his face. When it cleared, Raen stood in front of him, sword still stabbing the space where a

Roman had just been. The big man glanced down at the axe.

"Do what you must, lad, and quickly," he breathed before he parried a blow and turned to a new assailant.

Tormod gripped the handle with both his hands and sighted along its edge. Thora's eyes had rolled back in her head and the great diamond was growing brighter. Though he couldn't hear what she said, he knew that her vengeance had driven her mad. He could not let his clan be slaughtered, not even for his sister—the one he had saved all those centuries ago.

*Forgive me, Thora.*

He hurled the axe, straight and true, and knocked the diamond from her grasp.

Thora cried out as she clutched her mangled hand to her chest.

Tormod watched the Eye skitter along the ground, only to see it come to a stop against a worn, hobnail boot. The centurion looked down in astonishment but recovered quickly. He bent down and snatched it up, its golden sparkles dancing across his pale face. The Roman's delight sent a streak of cold into

Tormod's stomach, but the undead victory was short-lived. A broad blade cleaved the creature in two from head to hip.

"*Gavin*," Tormod muttered.

Before the golden jewel could hit the ground, the mortal spun and hit it with the flat of his sword. It sailed through the air directly at Tormod's face, and he caught it with one hand. Though the tangle of bodies around him had thickened, he caught a glance of Thora. She was frenetically shoving warriors this way and that, trying to see the ground. The eyes that had once sparkled with mischief, now glittered with blind hatred.

It was time to end this.

"Freyja," Tormod said as he lifted the diamond above his head, directly into the moonlight. "Open your eye and see those who would harm the innocent." As though she'd heard him over the din, his sister suddenly stopped and stared at him. "Do as you will with them."

The moon turned golden, and funneled a single, enormous shaft of light down over Tormod. Icy heat poured over him and through him, and gathered inside the heart of the diamond. Jema had given her life for this moment. If need be, Tormod would give his. The chaos would be defeated.

Power exploded from the jewel as it reflected thousands of shafts of light, which shot out from it to skewer every Roman on the island. But rather than fall into ash heaps, they exploded into balls of dust. The highlanders all around swung their weapons through the gray clouds. Shouts of astonishment replaced the clash of weapons.

Tormod saw a huge shaft slam into Gavin McShane, who was propelled through the air into the ocean. The mortal dropped and disappeared under the churning waves. Though Tormod peered through the radiance, trying to see if he resurfaced, the sea remained empty.

As a strange silence settled on the island, Thora looked at Tormod through the curtain of light. Their eyes met as her face turned gray and began to blow away in the bitter wind.

"You are my brother, and you have killed me."

He shook his head. "I've freed you, little sister. Go with my love."

Tormod made himself watch as the light destroyed Fenella Ivar's body, and released the white mist of Thora's spirit. It swirled for a moment over the undead female's ashen remains before it flew up into the night sky. For a moment he thought he heard Thora's voice whisper his name, and then she was gone.

The golden torque fell atop the pile of her ashes. All of its jewels had been burnt black. The blinding light shafts vanished as if they had never been, and Freyja's Eye closed.

Tormod dropped to the ground beside Jema. The diamond tumbled from his hand and rolled away to the edge of the sea well. He was still alive. For the first time he understood why Rachel had been so furious when she had been awakened and found Evander dead.

"Why did you no' take me with her?" he shouted at the stars. "We did as you asked. I loved her. I have never asked you for anything and you took her still. You are pitiless monsters."

A shooting star flew down and landed delicately on the edge of the shell mound, shaping itself into the wraith-like form of a giant female who stood at least fifteen feet tall. She took three steps and loomed over Tormod, her golden eye staring down at him. The other eye, which looked white and blind, remained half-closed.

"Pitiless, are we?" She floated around him. "I have showered you with gifts, and brought your enemies to justice. There is yet more work to be done, son of Arn," the goddess said. "But when it is your time, I will welcome you into Asgard myself." She stooped low to scoop up the gem, but it passed through her ghostly hand. "Midgard frustrates me. I cannot take true form here. It seems I will need your lady again."

Freyja rose and leapt into the air, swiveling in midair to dive into Jema's body.

Jema jerked and dragged in a strangled breath before she rolled over and choked out sea water.

Tormod staggered to his feet. "No, please dinnae take her. Let her sleep. She has done enough for you."

Jema's possessed body reached for the Eye, which she held close as she got to her feet. "Your woman has a large hole in her head. That will not do." She reached back and rubbed the crushed skull, which filled out and healed. "You have pleased us, son of Arn. You and your beloved sacrificed all for the good of others."

Freyja passed her hands over Jema's body, flooding it with golden power. Tormod flinched as the magic rayed out and engulfed him, reaching into his chest. As the goddess stepped out of Jema's body, she pressed the Eye back into her face and grew back to her previous height. Her two golden eyes shone down on them and the magic ray faded.

"This mortal is now made your immortal mate, ever tied to your heart. She shall live for as long as you, son of Arn."

Without another word the goddess flew up like a shooting star, and scattered herself among the heavens.

Jema stood looking down at her body with astonishment and then at him. "But I drowned," she said, sounding utterly bewildered. "I died. How can I be immortal now?"

"Freyja is very generous," he said. Then he seized her and kissed her until they were both shaking. "Oh, my lass. I thought I would have to end myself to be with you again."

"No talking of suicide, please." She touched his cheek, and then eagerly looked around them. "Where's Gavin?"

As the clan gathered round, Tormod pulled her close. He quietly told her what had happened, and then held her as she wept. When at last she lifted her head, he kissed her brow.

"I would ask the goddess to return him to you," he said, "but I dinnae think she would. The Eye demands a life for a life."

"Gavin for Thora," she whispered and nodded. Then she sniffed and wiped her eyes.

"The black boats have sailed, milord," Evander said to Lachlan. "Shall we give chase?"

All eyes turned to the laird, who shook his head. "There's been enough killing for one day."

"I've not yet made my apologies, my lord," Tormod said. He bowed his head. "I ken I did wrong, and I can only ask for your pardon."

"Pardon given, Viking." Lachlan glanced at the remnant ash left behind by the Romans. "So this is the work of Freyja's Eye. Efficient. We should speak respectfully of the Norse gods hence, I reckon."

Tormod grinned. "'Tis always best, my lord."

## Chapter Twenty-One

WHILE HE WAITED for the men to return with Fenella and the Eye, Quintus returned to his chamber to check on Bryn, who remained cold and still under the blanket. The little color she'd possessed had drained from her flesh, leaving her deathly pale. He lifted her upper lip to see the newly-formed fangs descending from her pallet.

"You shall become the first," he told her as he held her stiff hand in his. "I will train you to use your gifts to serve the Ninth, and to turn other women into undead. You will be the mother of our great change." He stroked her plump cheek. "But you will not wear the uniform. You will do as you know so well. I will send you to seduce rather than fight. You shall be the first of our legion whores."

Outside his chamber came the sound of commotion, and Quintus went out to learn the cause of it. A centurion with half of his face burned black hobbled toward him, supported by two of the deck hands.

"What has happened?" Quintus demanded.

"All the men are gone," the centurion said, his voice distorted by the deep injury. "One of the McDonnels used the jewel to burn them. Only I and two others survived because we ran for the water."

That meant nearly three hundred of his finest soldiers were dust. Defeat—once again crushing—at the hands of the McDonnels. Now they possessed the Eye, which could be used against the Ninth to wipe them from existence.

Through lips that barely moved, he said, "Take him and the other two below, and give them enough blood to heal."

Quintus went up on deck, where he ordered the crew to weigh anchor. To the captain, he said, "Set sail for Staffa. I want to be back at the stronghold in two days."

Still furious, he went to the cargo hold to select a thrall for Bryn to use once she woke from her transformation. The mortals brought on board had been first enthralled, so his presence made them rouse with welcoming smiles. Quintus chose a large, strapping farm hand and took him to the chamber, where he had him lay beside Bryn.

"She is dead, milord," the man mentioned, and then gasped as the plump woman rolled atop him. "Mistress, you are alive. How may I serve?"

Bryn smiled like a happy cherub at Quintus, who nodded, and then sank her fangs into his neck.

FEELING numb and never more alone in his life, Gavin watched his sister go off with the Viking and his clan. They weren't even going to look for his body. That was how relieved she was to be shut of him. He sat in silence against the rocks and stared down into the well, finally dropping his camouflage once they had sailed away from the skerry.

God, but it had gone completely to shite.

He forced himself to go to the spot where Thora had died, and picked up the ruined torque. He looked into its blackened, lifeless eye jewels, and then flung it into the sea.

As he pushed his hand into the heap of ash that was all that remained of her, Gavin finally wept—for the young shieldmaiden marked by the gods, for the sister that he'd lost, and eventually for himself. The gray stuff trickled through his fingers, dry and gritty, to blow away on the wind.

He had loved Thora, sensing in her a kindred warrior, a fearless woman bent on her mission. But he had learned too late that nothing would stand between her and her self-destructive vengeance, particularly him. He had loved his sister and searched for her, but obviously not she for him. All those months of caring for him and talk of Edinburg, it must have been guilt at work. He couldn't blame her for wanting to live her own life. But the thought of how quickly she must have started her new life—to have earned such a place in the Viking's clan—stabbed him in the gut.

Gavin finally stood and dusted the last bits of ash from his hands. He walked down to where he had hidden the dory he'd used to bring Thora to the island, and pushed it off the rocks and into the water. Though he might have followed the clan's boat, he took a different direction.

It was time to find his place in this world. For the first time, he wouldn't be bound to his twin sister's life. Nor would he offer his heart to another woman. He didn't need anyone.

Gavin thought of all the things he'd wanted to do while he'd been dying. It was time to go and do them.

## Chapter Twenty-Two

SOME WEEKS AFTER returning the Eye to the goddess, Tormod rode with Jema to the edge of the highland forest, where they tethered their horses and walked the rest of the way. Seeing what would become her dig site in the future gave Jema a sense of coming full-circle. She stayed far back from the edge, however, as her lover placed a sheaf of wildflowers over the crypt where Thora had been buried.

"Someday I hope to see you again, Sister," he said. "Until then, dinnae steal any more body parts from the goddess." He glanced back at her. "'Tis a chance to go back. We could jump in and come out on the other side in your time."

"There's nothing left there for me now." As she gazed off into the distance, Jema spotted a used trail and pointed it out to Tormod. "Someone's been here recently."

They followed the path to an empty hunting lodge near a river, and the moment they walked inside Jema closed her eyes and breathed in.

"Gavin was here." She looked around until she spotted his jacket, and grabbed it, hugging it for a moment. "This is where he must have been living before he met Thora. He would have loved roughing it."

They lingered in the little lodge as Jema picked up some of the crude tools and imagined Gavin's big hands using them. She sat on the low straw bed, and ran her hand over an old blue and green tartan that covered it. But as always when she thought of her brother, she couldn't help but wonder if he'd searched for her. Or maybe he thought she had died. She sighed as she got up and decided she would never know. Though she left everything else as they had found it, she took the jacket.

When they walked back they stopped by Thora's grave.

"Some nights I have the strangest dreams about him," Jema said. "He's working on a boat catching fish with a long rope with lots of hooks. Or he's building a house in the middle of a field. They seem so real it's hard to remember that he died." She nodded down at the pit. "Maybe he's in the next place."

"That doesnae sound strange to me," Tormod told her as he took her hand. "I know my sister's soul is at peace. At times I dream of her, always as a young girl, running through the glens on Skye. Now come. Since you dinnae wish to return to the future, there is something more I would show you."

Jema tucked her arm through his, and followed him back to the horses, which they mounted and rode north. Tormod finally reined in his gelding as they approached a large clearing with a primitive stone wall encircling it. A stream crossed the back of the glade, and several fruit trees formed a small orchard to one side of it. Jema brought her horse to a stop next to his.

"This is a lovely spot." Large stones, half-buried in the grass, were scattered in a circular pattern. “There aren’t any oak trees, so I’m guessing it’s not a portal.”

“I cannae tell you. ’Tis older than the clan. Mayhap it belonged to the very first Pritani to come here.” Tormod took out a curved piece of corroded metal, and handed it to her. “A hunter found this near the stones. Do you ken what it may have been?”

“It looks like an axe head.” She studied it for a moment. “Late Bronze Age, maybe. It’s a beautiful piece.” She met his gaze. “Tormod, what is this place?”

“’Tis ours. The laird is giving it to us.” He nodded toward the stones. “We might build a house there, once you’ve finished your dig. I’ll map the site, and help you with the work. Lachlan asked only that you tell him of what you find, for he has always been curious about it.”

Jema laughed. “I’ll bet.” She studied the land again. “This would be a wonderful place to have a summer cottage, but I like living at Dun Aran. I like being part of the clan.”

“As do I.” He leaned over to give her a kiss. “Now all you must do is marry me.” He dismounted, and helped her down. “Today.”

Jema wriggled against him. "What's your hurry? We don't have to be back at the castle until tonight. We could stay here and have a romp on our new land."

"I think no'." He nodded past her.

Jema turned to see Lachlan and Kinley emerge from the stream, followed by more McDonnels. Bhaltair and Cailean came out of the woods with other druids carrying baskets of food and blankets to spread on the ground. A little druidess skipped beside the old druid, her hair decorated with mistletoe, and a crown of the same in her hands. Neac and the Uthars hailed them as they carried up the casks of ale and whiskey. Diana started toward them, a long blue gown draped over her forearm. Rachel kept pace with her by trotting, her arms filled with flowers from the gardens at Dun Aran.

Jema laughed with delight. "This is our wedding?"

"Aye," Tormod said and took her hand. "Now come and make me the happiest of men."

THE END

• • • • •

Another Immortal Highlander awaits you in Gavin (Immortal Highlander Book 5).

For a sneak peek, turn the page.

## Sneak Peek

*Gavin (Immortal Highlander Book 5)*

Excerpt

# CHAPTER ONE

The pearl-capped sapphire waves of the North Sea lashed Gavin McShane as they buffeted the hull of the old boat. With practiced skill he guided the fisher into Scapa Flow, navigating his way through the boats and ships making passage between the islands that protected the wide but busy bay.

Overhead black wing-tipped gannets soared, diving now and then to scoop up fish to feed the screeching young waiting in their remote cliffside nests. Clear skies stretched wide and icy blue over the islands of Orkney, which resembled giant, rough-cut emeralds tumbling away from the north coast of Scotland. Gavin smiled a little as he passed other fishers that had yet to sail, or had returned with empty nets. Their crews cast envious looks at the mounds of cod heaped on the fisher's deck.

"See it and weep," Gavin murmured under his breath.

Being a twenty-first century man working on a medieval fishing boat had proven surprisingly satisfying. He no longer had to bother with phones, computers, cars, doctor's appointments, his walker or the disease that had been killing him in the future. Since time-traveling back to fourteenth-century Scotland, Gavin had enjoyed perfect health.

But he'd only achieved peace when he'd come to the islands.

Still, today's fine catch would pay his wages for three days, which would permit him the rest of the week to work on putting a roof on his house. He couldn't wait to finish it so he could move to Marr, the little jewel of an island he'd found off the coast of Hrossey.

"McShane," Bjarke Moller said as he came to join him at the helm. He was one of the three brothers who owned the boat. A burly man with strong arms roped by hard muscle and deep scars, he devoted himself to three pleasures in life: fishing, drinking and wenching. "Kron says you're no' to the alehouse with us. 'Tis true?"

"The salr needs work," Gavin replied. He now spoke without thinking in a thickened version of his natural brogue, but he still hesitated on some of the islander slang. "I can drink any day. I cannae sleep in my house without a roof."

"But you build on *Marr*, man?" That came from Silje Rowe, one of the net casters. The reedy, perpetually worried man touched the little wooden fish charm he wore around his neck. "No man goes near that island. 'Tis cursed."

"Och, aye, 'tis haunted by the ghost wench," Bjarke said and rolled his eyes. "She wears a torn blue gown and floats about the glen flashing her teats and arse. What does she now, steal men's souls, or eat them? I cannae recall."

"Dinnae jest about the Blue Lady of Marr," Silje warned. He clutched his talisman tightly, and lowered his voice to a whisper. "'Tis said she seeks vengeance for her tribe. They were massacred by blood-drinkers."

Gavin generally didn't mind listening to the fishermen's tall tales, but this one reminded him too much of the reason he had come to the islands to disappear. "I should see to the haul now."

"Aye, do," Bjarke said and took his place at the helm. "Silje, we're nearly to dock. Stop your havering and go ready the *vind-áss*."

*Windlass*, Gavin silently translated, the pulley and rope system that they used to lift their heavy haul. When he'd first arrived in Orkney the islander's odd hodgepodge of Scottish and Norse had forced him to say little until he built a rough working vocabulary. He'd probably never learn all of the slang, so he focused on words related to fish, the sea, and his work on the boat.

The crew got busy as they docked by the fish monger's pier. Hoisting the burgeoning nets meant hand-cranking the windlass before they swung the cod over to empty them into waiting carts. Once the catch was offloaded, the men worked together as a brigade to sluice the upper deck clean with buckets of salt water. Then they hung the thistle-hemp nets to dry. The day's tasks finished, the crew lined up to be paid by Bjarke, who promised them more work at the end of the week.

As the newest deck hand Gavin was always the last to be paid, but this time Bjarke handed him a few extra coins. "What's this?"

"Kron and Temmick and I want you to come on regular and captain the boat." Before Gavin could say anything the big man lifted his hand. "You do the work of three men, the crew respects you, and you've a nose for grand catches. 'Tis strange, for you're a highlander, but we think you've the spine for it. If our luck holds, we'll be building another boat. We'll want you ready for when the herring begin to run."

Gavin wanted to refuse. As a member of the crew he remained relatively anonymous.

But he liked working for the Mollers. He also needed to earn a living, and there were worse ways than spending every day out at sea.

"If you'll give me the time to put a roof on my salr, then aye." He took the big man's hand and nodded as they shook on it. "My thanks, Bjarke."

He had to trot to make the ferry that circled the bay to deliver people and supplies to the homes on the smaller islands. Gavin was the only one to disembark at Marr, and as he did he could feel the weight of the other passengers' gazes on his shoulders.

Stepping off onto the island's only dock, which was old but sturdy, he shouldered his pack and headed for the forest. Reaching the spot he'd chosen to build his house meant crossing the glen Silje claimed was haunted, although Gavin had never spotted anyone there. He liked to bathe in the fairy pool near the trees, and sometimes he jogged along the perimeter to stretch his legs. He'd been coming here for six months and hadn't seen anything but deer, rabbits and the funny-looking broad-beaked puffins who nested on the rocks.

Whether the ghost stole souls or ate them, she didn't seem very interested in his.

• • • • •

Buy *Gavin (Immortal Highlander Book 5)* Now

## DO ME A FAVOR?

You can make a big difference.

Reviews are the most powerful tools I have when it comes to getting attention for my books. Much as I'd like it, I don't have the financial muscle of a New York publisher. I can't take out full page ads in the newspaper—not yet, anyway.

But I do have something much more powerful. It's something that those publishers would kill for: **a committed and loyal group of readers.**

Honest reviews of my books help bring them to the attention of other readers. If you've enjoyed this book I would so appreciate it if you could spend a few minutes leaving a review—any length you like.

Thank you so much!

# MORE BOOKS BY HH

For a complete, up-to-date book list, visit HazelHunter.com/books.

Get notifications of new releases and special promotions by joining my newsletter!

# Glossary

Here are some brief definitions to help you navigate the medieval world of the Immortal Highlanders.

Abyssinia - ancient Ethiopia
acolyte - novice druid in training
addled - confused
advenae - Roman citizen born of freed slave parents
Ægishjálmr - the Helm of Awe, a magical sigil
afterlife - what happens after death
animus attentus - Latin for "listen closely"
apotheoses - highest points in the development of something
Aquilifer - standard bearer in a Roman legion
arse - ass

auld - old

Ave - Latin for "Hail"

aye - yes

bairn - child

Baltic – Scottish slang for very cold

banger - explosion

banshee in a bannock - making a mountain out of a molehill

barrow - wheelbarrow

bastart - bastard

bat - wooden paddle used to beat fabrics while laundering

battering ram - siege device used to force open barricaded entries and other fortifications

battle madness - Post Traumatic Stress Disorder

bawbag - scrotum

Belgia - Belgium

birlinn - medieval wooden boat propelled by sails and oars

blaeberry - European fruit that resembles the American blueberry

blind - cover device

blood kin - genetic relatives

bonny - beautiful

boon - gift or favor

brambles - blackberry bushes
bran'y - brandy
Brank's bridle mask - iron muzzle in an iron framework that enclosed the head
Britannia - Latin for "Britain"
brownie - Scottish mythical benevolent spirit that aids in household tasks but does not wish to be seen
buckler - shield
Caledonia - ancient Scotland
caligae - type of hobnailed boots worn by the Roman legion
cannae - can't
cannel - cinnamon
canny - shrewd, sharp
catch-fire - secret and highly combustible Pritani compound that can only be extinguished by sand
Centurio - Latin for "Centurions"
century - Roman legion unit of 100 men
chatelaine - woman in charge of a large house
Chieftain - second highest-ranking position within the clan; the head of a specific Pritani tribe
choil - unsharpened section of a knife just in front of the guard

Choosing Day - Pritani manhood ritual during which adolescent boys are tattooed and offer themselves to empowering spirits
chow - food
cistern - underground reservoir for storing rain water
claymore - two-edged broadsword
clout - strike
cohort - Roman legion tactical military unit of approximately 500 men
cold pantry - underground cache or room for the storage of foods to be kept cool
comely - attractive
conclave - druid ruling body
conclavist - member of the druid ruling body
conkers – horse chestnuts
contubernium - squad of eight men; the smallest Roman legion formation
COP - Command Observation Post
cosh - to bash or strike
couldnae - couldn't
counter - in the game of draughts, a checker
courses - menstrual cycle
cow - derogatory term for woman
Coz - cousin
croft - small rented farm

cudgel - wooden club
da - dad
daft - crazy
dappled - animal with darker spots on its coat
defendi altus - Latin for “defend high"
detail - military group assignment
dinnae - don’t
dirk – a long-bladed dagger
disincarnate - commit suicide
diviner - someone who uses magic or extra sensory perception to locate things
doesnae - doesn’t
dories - small boats used for ship to shore transport
draughts - board game known as checkers in America
drawers - underpants
drivel - nonsense
drover - a person who moves herd animals over long distances
dung - feces
EDC - Every Day Carry, a type of knife
excavators - tunnel-diggers
fack - fuck
facking - fucking
fankle – knot

faodail - lucky find
fash - feel upset or worried
fathom - understand
fere spectare - Latin for "about face"
ferret out - learn
festers - becomes infected
fetters - restraints
fibula - Roman brooch or pin for fastening clothes
filching - stealing
fisher - boat
fishmonger - person who sells fish for food
floor-duster - Pritani slang for druid
foam-mouth - rabies
fougou – a stone-walled vault built underground for storage and other purposes
Francia - France
Francian - French
free traders - smugglers
frenzy - mindless, savagely aggressive, mass-attack behavior caused by starving undead smelling fresh blood
fripperies - showy or unnecessary ornament
Germania - Germany
god-ridden - possessed
Great Design - secret druid master plan

greyling - species of freshwater fish in the salmon family
gut rot - cancer of the bowel
hasnae - hasn't
heid doon arse up - battle command: head down, ass up
Hetlandensis - oldest version of the modern name Shetland
Hispania - Roman name for the Iberian peninsula (modern day Portugal and Spain)
hold - below decks, the interior of a ship
holk - type of medieval ship used on rivers and close to coastlines as a barge
hoor - whore
huddy - stupid, idiotic
impetus - Latin for "attack"
incarnation - one of the many lifetimes of a druid
isnae - isn't
jeeked - extremely tired
Joe - GI Joe shortened, slang for American soldier
jotunn - Norse mythic giantess
justness - justice
kelpie - water spirit of Scottish folklore, typically taking the form of a horse,

reputed to delight in the drowning of travelers

ken - know

kennings – compound expressions in Old Norse poetry with metaphorical meanings

kirtle - one piece garment worn over a smock

kona – Old Norse for woman

kuks - testicles

kyn-ligr – Old Norse for strange, wondrous

lad - boy

laird - lord

lapstrake - method of boat building where the hull planks overlap

larder - pantry

lass - girl

league - distance measure of approximately three miles

Legio nota Hispania - Latin name for The Ninth Legion

loggia - open-side room or house extension that is partially exposed to the outdoors

Losh – Scottish expletive meaning "Lord"

magic folk - druids

mam - mom

mannish - having characteristics of a man

mantle - loose, cape-like cloak worn over garments
mayhap - maybe
milady - my lady
milord - my lord
missive - message
mormaer - regional or provincial ruler, second only to the Scottish king
motte - steep-sided man-made mound of soil on which a castle was built
mustnae - must not
naught - nothing
no' - not
Norrvegr - ancient Norway
Noto - Latin for "Attention"
Optia - rank created for female Roman Legion recruit Fenella Ivar
Optio - second in command of a Roman legion century
orachs - slang term for chanterelle mushrooms
orcharders - slang for orchard farmers
ovate - Celtic priest or natural philosopher
palfrey - docile horse
paludamentum - cloak or cape worn fastened at one shoulder by Romans military commanders

parati - Latin for “ready"

parched - thirsty, dry

parlay - bargain

penchants - strong habits or preferences

perry - fermented pear juice

Pict - member of an ancient people inhabiting northern

pure done in – exhausted

Scotland in Roman times

pillion - seated behind a rider

pipes - bagpipes

pisspot - chamber pot, toilet

plumbed - explored the depth of

poppet - doll

poppy juice - opium

pottage - a thick, stew-like soup of meat and vegetables

pox-ridden - infected with syphilis

praefectus - Latin for “prefect”

Prefect - senior magistrate or governor in the ancient Roman world

Pritani - Britons (one of the people of southern Britain before or during Roman times)

privy - toilet

quim - woman's genitals

quinie – young woman
quoits - medieval game like modern ring toss
repulsus - Latin for “drive back"
rescue bird - search and rescue helicopter
roan - animal with mixed white and pigmented hairs
roo - to pluck loose wool from a sheep
rumble - fight
salr - Old Norse for a house consisting of one room
Sassenachs - Scottish term for English people
scunner - source of irritation or strong dislike
sea stack - column of eroded cliff or shore rock standing in the sea
Seid - Norse magic ritual
selkie - mythical creature that resembles a seal in the water but assumes human form on land
semat - undershirt
seneschal - steward or major-domo of a medieval great house
shield-maiden – a Norsewoman who choses to fight as a warrior
shouldnae - shouldn't
shroud - cloth used to wrap a corpse before burial
skald – storyteller

skelp - strike, slap, or smack

skin work - tattoos

skuddie – naked

smalls - men's underwear

SoCal - slang for southern California

solar - rooms in a medieval castle that served as the family's private living and sleeping quarters

spellfire - magically-created flame

spellmark - visible trace left behind by the use of magic

spew - vomit

spindle - wooden rod used in spinning

squared - made right

stad - Scots Gaelic for "halt"

staunch weed - yarrow

stupit - stupid

Svitiod - ancient Sweden

swain - young lover or suitor

swived - have sexual intercourse with

taobh - Scots Gaelic for "Flank"

tempest - storm

tester - canopy over a bed

the pox - smallpox

thickhead - dense person

thimblerig - shell game

thrawn - stubborn
’tis - it is
’tisnt - it isn’t
toadies - lackeys
tonsure - shaved crown of the head
torque – a metal neck ring
TP - toilet paper
traills - slaves
trencher - wooden platter for food
trews - trousers
trials - troubles
Tribune - Roman legionary officer
tuffet - low seat or footstool
’twas - it was
’twere - it was
’twill - it will
’twould - it would
tyre – tire
Underground – Scottish subway system
Vesta - Roman goddess of the hearth
wand-waver - Pritani slang for druid
warband - group of warriors sent together on a specific mission
wasnae - wasn’t
water elf sickness – a medieval-era disease

now believed to be chicken pox, endocarditis, or measles

wee - small

wench - girl or young woman

wenching - womanizing or chasing women for the purposes of seduction

white plague - tuberculosis

whoreson - insult; the son of a prostitute

widdershins - in a direction contrary to the sun's course, considered as unlucky; counter-clockwise.

willnae - will not

woad - plant with leaves that produce blue dye

wouldnae - would not

ye - you

yer – your

## Pronunciation Guide

A selection of the more challenging words in the Immortal Highlander series.

Bhaltair Flen - BAHL-ter Flen
Bjarke Moller - YAR-kay MOH-lah
Black Cuillin - COO-lin
Cailean Lusk - KAH-len Luhsk
Dun Aran - doon AIR-uhn
Evander Talorc - ee-VAN-der TAY-lork
faodail - FOOT-ill
Fiona Marphee - fee-O-nah MAR-fee
Kron Moller - KRAHN MOH-lah
Lachlan McDonnel - LOCK-lin mik-DAH-nuhl
Loch Sìorraidh - Lock SEEO-rih
Neacal Uthar - NIK-ul OO-thar

Seoc Talorc - SHOK TAY-lork

Silje Rowe - seel-JAY ROH

Temmick Moller - TEM-mick MOH-lah

Tharaen Aber - theh-RAIN AY-burr

Thora Liefson - THOR-ah LEEF-sun

Tormod Liefson - TORE-mod LEEF-sun

# Dedication

*For Mr. H.*

# Copyright

# Making Magic

Welcome to Making Magic, a little section at the end of the book where I can give readers a glimpse at what I do. It's not edited and my launch team doesn't read it because it's kind of a last minute thing. Therefore typos will surely follow.

The way of the series is akin to a tightrope. In any book, let alone a series, a writer hopes that readers connect with the characters. They are the heart and mind of the story. Plot, while critical, is the skeletal structure. The story won't go anywhere without it. But it is the hero and heroine that make or break it. And this is where the tightrope comes in.

A series promises to deliver more of the same, whether the authors says so or not. One immortal highlander must follow another or reader expectations are not met. But the balancing trick is to keep it from feeling repetitive. Each story in this series, though all set in the same world with the same ground rules, focuses on a different couple. So my challenge comes in creating compelling people whose journey to happiness doesn't cover old ground. Lucky for me, the McDonnel clan is big. :) And the possible paths to happiness are many.

I've already been asked if I'll be adding to the series. I'm committed to at least five, but feeling more and more like six or seven might be the magic number. If it's fresh and you're enjoying it, then I am totally up for it. If you have a minute, and feel like dropping me a line to let me know, I'd really appreciate hearing from you.

Thank you for reading, thank you for reviewing, and I'll see you between the covers soon.

XOXO,

Hazel

Los Angeles, November 2017

Read Me

Like Me

Grab My Next Book?